It's Time Again For . . .

MOVIE MANIA!

Why be a fan when you can be a star? Cast yourself as a winner in the new movie trivia hit, TRIVIA MANIA! And you can start right now down the yellow brick road toward trivia superstardom with the following cinema stumpers:

—Who plays James Dean's father in *Rebel Without a Cause*?
—In Joan Rivers' *Rabbit Test*, who plays the world's first pregnant man?
—In what 1980 film does Richard Gere peddle his wares to wealthy women?
—What is the real name of the dog known as Benji?
—Name Humphrey Bogart's character in *The Treasure of the Sierra Madre*.
—The Three Stooges co-starred in a film with Clark Gable and Joan Crawford. True or false?
—Spencer Tracy plays a one-armed man in what 1954 movie?
—Who plays Gary Cooper's young deputy in *High Noon*?
—What was the name of the card game played by the ballplayers in *Bang the Drum Slowly*?
—E.T. was fond of what brand of beer?

For the answers to these and more than a thousand other fascinating questions, keep on reading and surrender yourself to TRIVIA MANIA!

MOVIES VOLUME II

TRIVIA Mania

BY XAVIER EINSTEIN

ZEBRA BOOKS
KENSINGTON PUBLISHING CORP.

This book could not have been possible without the work of Howard M. Singer.

ZEBRA BOOKS

are published by

Kensington Publishing Corp.
475 Park Avenue South
New York, N.Y. 10016

First printing: August 1984

Printed in the United States of America

TRIVIA MANIA:
Movies (Vol. II)

1) In Hitchcock's *The Lady Vanishes*, who portrays the vanished lady?

2) In *Bonzo Goes to College*, Ronald Reagan drinks a potion and is transformed into a chimpanzee. True or false?

3) Who was most often the female foil in the Marx Brothers' films?

4) Who directed the film *Some Like It Hot*?

5) What is the name of the most famous pterodactyl in movies?

6) Jeff Bridges and Barry Brown play drifters on the run during the Civil War in what 1972 film?

. . . Answers

1. Dame May Whitty

2. False

3. Margaret Dumont

4. Billy Wilder

5. Rodan

6. *Bad Company*

QUESTIONS

7) What documentary featured George Harrison and Bob Dylan in concert to raise money for an impoverished nation?

8) What is the real name of the dog known as Benji?

9) What film features the nasty Blue Meanies?

10) What writer created the detective Philip Marlowe?

11) Who plays the lead in *The Ghost and Mr. Chicken*?

12) Robert Redford and Dustin Hoffman play *Washington Post* reporters Woodward and Bernstein in what film?

13) In *Still of the Night*, Roy Scheider plays a psychiatrist. His mother in the film is Jessica Tandy. What is her profession?

14) They teamed up in 1930 in *Min and Bill*, and again in 1933 in *Tugboat Annie*. Who are they?

15) Name Humphrey Bogart's character in *The Treasure of the Sierra Madre*.

16) The Three Stooges co-starred in a film with Clark Gable and Joan Crawford. True or false?

17) What Norman Mailer World War II novel came to the screen in 1958?

. . . Answers

7. *The Concert for Bangladesh*

8. Higgins

9. *Yellow Submarine*

10. Raymond Chandler

11. Don Knotts

12. *All the President's Men*

13. A psychiatrist

14. Marie Dressler and Wallace Beery

15. Fred C. Dobbs

16. True (*Dancing Lady*)

17. *The Naked and the Dead*

18) Jackie Coogan became a huge child star after appearing in which film with Charlie Chaplin?

19) Who plays Ann-Margret's father in the 1963 musical comedy *Bye Bye Birdie*?

20) Spencer Tracy and Frederic March are modeled after what two famous attorneys arguing the theory of evolution in the 1960 film *Inherit the Wind*?

21) Who plays the precocious child in *The Goodbye Girl*?

22) What is the destination of the ship in *Airplane II: The Sequel*?

23) Elroy "Crazylegs" Hirsch plays himself in *Crazylegs*. True or false?

24) Cyd Charisse is a Russian bureaucrat who falls in love with capitalist movie director Fred Astaire in what musical remake of *Ninotchka?*

25) What Cole Porter song plays over the credits at the end of Woody Allen's *Everything You Always Wanted to Know About Sex (But Were Afraid to Ask)*?

26) Who plays the lead in the 1971 film *The Projectionist*?

27) What is Barbra Streisand's profession in *The Owl and the Pussycat*?

... *Answers*

18. *The Kid*

19. Paul Lynde

20. Clarence Darrow and William Jennings Bryan

21. Quinn Cummings

22. The moon

23. True

24. *Silk Stockings*

25. "Let's Misbehave"

26. Chuck McCann

27. A prostitute

28) Who plays the idealistic writer in *The Petrified Forest*?

29) Ray Walston is the devil, but who is his lusty servant in *Damn Yankees*?

30) Who won an Oscar in 1972 for her portrayal of Sally Bowles in the film *Cabaret*?

31) Frank Sinatra is a hard-nosed detective in what 1968 movie?

32) Who spoke the famous line "I want to be alone"?
    a. Greta Garbo
    b. Joan Fontaine
    c. Vivien Leigh
    d. Bette Davis

33) What city goes up in flames in *Gone With the Wind*?

34) In what 1971 film later retitled *Never Give an Inch*, does Paul Newman display Henry Fonda's dismembered arm as an act of defiance to striking loggers?

35) E.T. was fond of what brand of beer?

36) In *Sergeant York*, Gary Cooper appears briefly in women's clothing. True or false?

37) What group wrote and performed the music in *Saturday Night Fever*?

. . . Answers

28. Leslie Howard

29. Gwen Verdon

30. Liza Minnelli

31. *The Detective*

32. a

33. Atlanta

34. *Sometimes a Great Notion*

35. Coors

36. False

37. The Bee Gees

QUESTIONS

38) Who directed the panoramic film *Barry Lyndon*?

39) Who plays President Truman in *Give 'Em Hell, Harry*?

40) Gene Hackman plays a surveillance expert in what 1974 film?

41) In *The Day the Earth Stood Still*, what was the name of Michael Rennie's robot?

42) Who played Major Dundee in the film of the same name?

43) Name the dog in the *Thin Man* series.

44) In what movie were Dan Aykroyd and John Belushi siblings?

45) Who played Lincoln in the 1940 film *Abe Lincoln in Illinois*?

46) What did Fred MacMurray discover in *The Absent-Minded Professor*?

47) Who played Sidney Greenstreet's gunsel in *The Maltese Falcon*?

48) Who was Cosmo in *Singin' in the Rain*?

. . . *Answers*

38. Stanley Kubrick

39. James Whitmore

40. *The Conversation*

41. Gort

42. Charlton Heston

43. Asta

44. *The Blues Brothers*

45. Raymond Massey

46. Flubber

47. Elisha Cook, Jr.

48. Donald O'Connor

QUESTIONS

49) Billy Dee Williams and James Earl Jones star as baseball players in what movie?

50) Cloris Leachman portrays what character in *Young Frankenstein*?

51) In *Witness for the Prosecution*, Charles Laughton is the defense attorney, Elsa Lanchester his nurse, and Marlene Dietrich the wife of the defendant. Who is the defendant?

52) What film opens with the song "On Broadway" and closes with the song "Bye Bye Love"?

53) In what 1980 film does Richard Gere peddle his wares to wealthy women?

54) In which movie did Claudette Colbert maintain that her father was a "great piggybacker"?

55) Who plays the senior senator in *Mr. Smith Goes to Washington*?

56) Who plays the lead in the *Mr. Moto* series?

57) What 1982 thriller features a little girl who talks to "TV people"?

58) Who directed *The Birth of a Nation*?

. . . Answers

49. *The Bingo Long Traveling All-Stars and Motor Kings*

50. Herr Blucher

51. Tyrone Power

52. *All That Jazz*

53. *American Gigolo*

54. *It Happened One Night*

55. Claude Rains

56. Peter Lorre

57. *Poltergeist*

58. D.W. Griffith

59) Name the two co-stars in *The Man Who Would be King*.

60) What comedy team starred in *Hellzapoppin* and *Crazy House*?

61) In *Apocalypse Now*, what actor literally "loses his head" in Martin Sheen's lap?

62) Who stars as the free-spirited woman in the 1960 film *Never on Sunday*?

63) Bo Derek and Dudley Moore make love to what classical piece in *10*?

64) Orson Welles' *Citizen Kane* was supposed to be based on what real-life character?

65) What all-pro basketball player appeared in the 1979 film *The Fish That Saved Pittsburgh*?

66) Zero Mostel romances little old ladies in order to bankroll a Broadway flop in *The Producers*. What character does Mostel play?

67) Who plays two parts in the 1937 version of *The Prisoner of Zenda*?

68) In 1975, Jeff Bridges appeared in two films. In one he played a cattle rustler, in the other a writer of westerns. Name the two movies.

. . . Answers

59. Michael Caine and Sean Connery

60. Olsen and Johnson

61. Frederick Forrest

62. Melina Mercouri

63. Ravel's "Bolero"

64. William Randolph Hearst

65. Julius Erving

66. Max Bialystock

67. Ronald Colman

68. *Rancho Deluxe* and *Hearts of the West*

69) Who stars in *The Buddy Holly Story*?

70) Burt Reynolds is a top Hollywood stuntman who is being challenged by a newcomer in *Hooper*. Who plays the tyro?

71) *Andy Warhol's Frankenstein* was filmed in 3-D. True or false?

72) In *Lord of the Flies*, what is the name of the character whose "specs" are used to start fires?

73) John Voight stars as a schoolteacher of black children in *Conrack*. Who plays his boss?

74) What John Ford film starring Henry Fonda as Wyatt Earp and Victor Mature as Doc Holliday ends with the gunfight at O.K. Corral?

75) Name the 1973 rock and roll documentary that features Chuck Berry, Bill Haley, Chubby Checker and Bo Diddly?

76) What 1972 film features a blind boy's romance with his wacky neighbor (Goldie Hawn)?

77) What was Dorothy's last name in *The Wizard of Oz*?

78) Who directed *The Boy Friend*?

79) Gene Kelly directed *Xanadu*. True or false?

. . . *Answers*

69. Gary Busey

70. Jan-Michael Vincent

71. True

72. Piggy

73. Hume Cronyn

74. *My Darling Clementine*

75. *Let the Good Times Roll*

76. *Butterflies Are Free*

77. Gale

78. Ken Russell

79. False

80) Who plays the hypnotist in the 1931 film *Svengali*?

81) Jack Lemmon and Lee Remick are hopeless alcoholics in what movie?

82) What visually beautiful film set in early twentieth century Texas features the love triangle of Richard Gere, Sam Shepard and Brooke Adams?

83) Charlton Heston portrays Michelangelo in what film?

84) In *Chariots of Fire*, the British track stars compete in the Olympics of what year?

85) Russian Hedy Lamarr falls for American reporter Clark Gable in what movie?

86) Jill Clayburgh is the first woman Supreme Court Justice in what film?

87) Do welding and hoofing mix? They do in Pittsburgh in what 1983 film?

88) Barbara Stanwyck won an Oscar for her role as a woman who overhears a murder plan on the telephone, only to discover that she is the intended victim. Name this movie.

89) *Bound for Glory* won an Oscar in what category?

. . . Answers

80. John Barrymore

81. *Days of Wine and Roses*

82. *Days of Heaven*

83. *The Agony and the Ecstasy*

84. 1924

85. *Comrade X*

86. *First Monday in October*

87. *Flashdance*

88. *Sorry, Wrong Number*

89. Cinematography

90) In *The Ghost and Mrs. Muir*, who is Mrs. Muir?

91) What 1976 film features Jodie Foster and Scott Baio in an all-kid gangster musical spoof?

92) What was the name of the business that sponsored *The Bad News Bears*?

93) Who stars as Mame in the 1974 film?

94) In *Monty Python and the Holy Grail*, John Cleese plays a mysterious wizard who is known by what name?

95) What kind of character did Peter Sellers play in *The Bobo*?

96) Ben Gazzara, John Cassavetes and Peter Falk take off to Europe when their best friend dies in what 1970 movie?

97) Who play *McCabe and Mrs. Miller*?

98) Who plays the lead in *Kill the Umpire*?

99) What drummer stars opposite Barbara Bach in the 1981 film *Caveman*?

100) Betty Grable, Lauren Bacall and Marilyn Monroe are all seeking eligible men in what movie?

101) Who stars in *The Fatal Glass of Beer*?

. . . Answers

90. Gene Tierney

91. *Bugsy Malone*

92. Chico's Bail Bonds

93. Lucille Ball

94. Tim

95. A singing matador

96. *Husbands*

97. Warren Beatty and Julie Christie

98. William Bendix

99. Ringo Starr

100. *How to Marry a Millionaire*

101. W.C. Fields

102) Name the two androids in *Star Wars*.

103) What were the two gangs in *West Side Story*?

104) Who won an Oscar for his portrayal of a POW suspected of being a German spy in *Stalag 17*?

105) What was the name of the duck in *Journey to the Center of the Earth*?

106) Sally Fields organizes a union in a cotton mill in what film?

107) Whom does Sam Shepard portray in *The Right Stuff*?

108) What actor played *Zorba the Greek*?

109) In the 1979 film, *Time After Time*, Malcolm McDowell pursues David Warner. What two characters are they supposed to be?

110) In which James Bond movie does Oddjob appear?

111) Jack Webb directed and starred in what 1957 film about a Marine boot camp?

112) What was Alex Karras' name in *Blazing Saddles*?

113) What actor said, "What we have here is a failure to communicate" in *Cool Hand Luke*?

. . . Answers

102. R2D2 and C3PO

103. The Sharks and the Jets

104. William Holden

105. Gertrude

106. *Norma Rae*

107. Chuck Yeager

108. Anthony Quinn

109. H.G. Wells and Jack the Ripper

110. *Goldfinger*

111. *The D.I.*

112. Mongo

113. Strother Martin

QUESTIONS

114) Who plays the troubled youth in *East of Eden*?

115) Who plays the college professor in *Animal House*?

116) In *The French Connection*, what is the name of the officer that Gene Hackman plays?

117) What Jim Henson film features Gelflings and Skeksies?

118) Who plays the lead in *Jim Thorpe — All American*?

119) Louise Fletcher won an Oscar for her portrayal of what character in *One Flew Over the Cuckoo's Nest*?

120) In Mel Brooks' *Silent Movie*, who speaks the only word in the entire film and what is the word?

121) Identify the speaker and the movie of the following line: "Ever been bit by a dead bee?"

122) Who stars in *Monsieur Verdoux* as a man who murders his wives for their money?

123) Name the male and female stars of *High Sierra*?

124) Who directed *Last Tango in Paris*?

125) What was the sequel to *Mister Roberts*?

. . . Answers

114. James Dean

115. Donald Sutherland

116. Popeye Doyle

117. *The Dark Crystal*

118. Burt Lancaster

119. Nurse Ratchet

120. Marcel Marceau and "No"

121. Walter Brennan in *To Have and Have Not*

122. Charles Chaplin

123. Humphrey Bogart and Ida Lupino

124. Bernardo Bertolucci

125. *Ensign Pulver*

126) Haley Mills makes her debut as a girl who witnesses a murder in what 1959 film?

127) Who plays Gunga Din in the movie of the same name?

128) Fred Astaire appears in a straight role in what movie about Australians awaiting the consequences of a nuclear war?

129) What musical group was featured in the 1965 film *Ferry Cross the Mersey*?

130) In what World War II movie does Robert Mitchum save German submarine commander Curt Jurgens by throwing him a rope?

131) Who plays Auntie Mame in the 1958 film?
    a. Rosalind Russell
    b. Lucille Ball
    c. Joan Crawford
    d. Pia Zadora

132) Who is the Vietnam vet pursued by the police in *First Blood*?

133) What classic sci-fi film features Walter Pidgeon, Anne Francis and Robby the Robot?

134) Chaplin's *The Gold Rush* takes place in San Francisco. True or false?

. . . Answers

126. *Tiger Bay*

127. Sam Jaffe

128. *On the Beach*

129. Gerry and the Pacemakers

130. *The Enemy Below*

131. a

132. Sylvester Stallone

133. *Forbidden Planet*

134. False (the Yukon)

QUESTIONS

135) What studio produced *Emil and the Detectives*?

136) Burt Lancaster plays a phony evangelist in what movie based on a Sinclair Lewis story?

137) What country is the setting for the 1983 film *The Year of Living Dangerously*?

138) In what movie did Paul Newman play Billy the Kid?

139) In *Little Big Man*, Chief Dan George played the leader of the Cheyennes and referred to his tribe by another name. What was the name?

140) Robin Williams played T.S. Garp in *The World According to Garp*. What does the T.S. stand for?

141) Who sings the score in Jonathan Livingston Seagull?

142) Who directed *A New Leaf*?
   a. Gene Saks
   b. Elaine May
   c. Richard Benjamin
   d. Neil Simon

143) In the 1939 film *Of Mice and Men*, who play George and Lenny?

. . . Answers

135. Disney

136. *Elmer Gantry*

137. Indonesia

138. *The Left-Handed Gun*

139. The Human Beings

140. Technical Sergeant

141. Neil Diamond

142. b

143. Burgess Meredith and Lon Chaney, Jr.

QUESTIONS

144) Sam Peckinpah did not direct which film?
   a. *The Life and Times of Judge Roy Bean*
   b. *Major Dundee*
   c. *The Ballad of Cable Hogue*
   d. *Straw Dogs*

145) Jack Nicholson is a masochist in what Roger Corman film?

146) What dancer plays Valentino in the 1977 film?

147) Tony Perkins and Tuesday Weld star as a wacked-out young couple up to no good in what 1968 film?

148) What 1971 movie features a scene of a woman who is murdered by being impaled with a giant phallic symbol?

149) The shark in *Jaws* terrorizes the inhabitants of the island of Nantucket. True or false?

150) Robert DeNiro and Robert Duvall are brothers in *True Confessions*. What are their professions?

151) Al Pacino robs a bank to pay for his lover's sex change operation in what film?

152) What 1979 Fassbinder film traces a woman's rise to power in postwar Germany?

. . . *Answers*

144. a

145. *The Little Shop of Horrors*

146. Rudolf Nureyev

147. *Pretty Poison*

148. *A Clockwork Orange*

149. False (Martha's Vineyard)

150. A priest and a detective

151. *Dog Day Afternoon*

152. *The Marriage of Maria Braun*

QUESTIONS

153) What "Faberge" blonde stars in the 1980 sci-fi movie *Saturn 3*?

154) Ricky Schroder cries his way through this remake of a Wallace Beery-Jackie Cooper movie. What movie?

155) Michael Caine and Christopher Reeve plot to scare Dyan Cannon to death in what film?

156) What Australian film culminates in a suicidal attack against the Turks in World War I?

157) Richard Dreyfuss is an ambitious Jewish kid out to make a fortune in what 1974 film?

158) In the movie *Chinatown*, who plays the little tough guy who slices off a bit of Jack Nicholson's nose?

159) What was the name of the card game played by the ballplayers in *Bang the Drum Slowly*?

160) In *The Big Chill*, what was the name of Kevin Kline's athletic footwear franchise?

161) *World Without Sun*, an Oscar-winning documentary in 1964, was directed by whom?

162) What Luis Bunuel production won the Academy Award for Best Foreign Film in 1972?

... *Answers*

153. Farrah Fawcett

154. *The Champ*

155. *Deathtrap*

156. *Gallipoli*

157. *The Apprenticeship of Duddy Kravitz*

158. Roman Polanski

159. Tegwar (The Entertaining Game Without Any Rules)

160. The Running Dog

161. Jacques Cousteau

162. The Discreet Charm of the Bourgeoisie

163) Although Barbara Eden starred in the 1964 film *The Brass Bottle*, she didn't play the genie. Who did?

164) Mike Nichols directed the film, Buck Henry wrote the screenplay, and Joseph Heller provided the novel for what black comedy?

165) Clark Gable vacillates between tough-girl Jean Harlow and genteel Rosalind Russell on a ship bound for Hong Kong in what film?

166) Sam Fuller wrote and directed the story of a journalist who goes into an insane asylum to unmask a killer and ends up going insane himself in what tense melodrama?

167) In *Diary of a Mad Housewife*, with whom does Carrie Snodgrass have an affair?

168) Peter Boyle stars as a hardhat bigot in what 1970 film?

169) Who is Andy Griffith's sidekick in *No Time for Sergeants*?

170) Richard Crenna is one of several astronauts stranded in space while agency head Gregory Peck tries to get a handle on things in what film?

171) In *On the Waterfront*, who plays union boss Johnny Friendly?

. . . *Answers*

163. Burl Ives

164. *Catch-22*

165. *China Seas*

166. *Shock Corridor*

167. Frank Langella

168. *Joe*

169. Nick Adams

170. *Marooned*

171. Lee J. Cobb

QUESTIONS

172) Who plays the lead in *The Unsinkable Molly Brown*?
 a. Debbie Reynolds
 b. Julie Andrews
 c. Audrey Hepburn
 d. Shirley Jones

173) What 1964 British film depicts the true story of a massacre of an English mission in Africa in 1879?

174) Jackie Gleason and Estelle Parsons head an American family in a communist nation who are accused of being spies in *Don't Drink the Water*. Who wrote the script?

175) Who stars in John Huston's film *Freud*?

176) What John Ford western features an all-star cast as it tells the story of three generations of pioneer families?

177) How many dalmatians are there in the Disney film?
 a. 76
 b. 101
 c. 99
 d. 1001
 e. 98

178) In what Frank Capra film does Gary Cooper inherit twenty million dollars and attempt to give it all away to needy families?

. . . Answers

172. a

173. *Zulu*

174. Woody Allen

175. Montgomery Clift

176. *How the West Was Won*

177. b

178. *Mr. Deeds Goes to Town*

QUESTIONS

179) Who are the two stars of the 1934 screwball comedy *Twentieth Century*?

180) Who stars as the wealthy socialite in *Platinum Blonde*?

181) Jimmy Cliff popularized reggae music with what 1973 Jamaican film?

182) Spencer Tracy plays a priest and Frank Sinatra is one of three convicts who help to rescue children from a volcano in what film?

183) Glen Ford is a seaman struggling to make it as a writer in *The Adventures of Martin Eden*. On whose book is this film based?

184) Better known as Perry Mason's secretary, she stars with Robert Young as a divorced mother-to-be in *And Baby Makes Three*. Name her.

185) What 1982 documentary consists of film clips and training films of U.S. propaganda about The Bomb?

186) Pat O'Brien co-starred with James Cagney in all but one of the following films. Which one?
   a. *Torrid Zone*
   b. *The Roaring Twenties*
   c. *The Fighting 69th*
   d. *Angels With Dirty Faces*

. . . Answers

179. Carole Lombard and John Barrymore

180. Jean Harlow

181. *The Harder They Come*

182. *The Devil at 4 O'Clock*

183. Jack London

184. Barbara Hale

185. *The Atomic Cafe*

186. b

187) *God Is My Co-Pilot*, with Raymond Massey and Dennis Morgan, is a tribute to what famous World War II airborne unit?

188) Who plays the private eye in *Tony Rome* and *The Lady in Cement*?

189) In *Kind Hearts and Coronets*, one member of an aristocratic house sets out to kill all the others to gain an inheritance. The star, Alec Guinness, plays how many roles in this black comedy?
    a. two
    b. three
    c. five
    d. eight

190) Who plays dancer Isadora Duncan in *The Loves of Isadora*?

191) From what movie is the song "Everybody's Talkin' "?

192) What former member of *Your Show of Shows* directed Doris Day and Brian Keith in *With Six You Get Eggroll*?
    a. Imogene Coca
    b. Howard Morris
    c. Sid Caesar
    d. Carl Reiner

. . . Answers

187. The Flying Tigers

188. Frank Sinatra

189. d

190. Vanessa Redgrave

191. *Midnight Cowboy*

192. b

193) Who plays the radio operator who has a breakdown onboard the submarine in *The Bedford Incident*?

194) Doris Day and Robert Morse star in *Where Were You When the Lights Went Out* in 1968. This movie is about what famous event?

195) "The pellet with the poison's in the vessel with the pestle." Name the film with this phrase, and the actor who tries to remember it.

196) Which of the following didn't appear in *The Dirty Dozen*?
  a. Lee Marvin
  b. John Cassavetes
  c. George Kennedy
  d. Robert Ryan

197) What was Clint Eastwood's first "spaghetti Western"?

198) In *The Professionals*, Ralph Bellamy hires four mercenaries, including Burt Lancaster and Lee Marvin, to rescue his wife from a Mexican bandit. Who plays the Mexican?

199) Jason Robards plays Bugs Moran in *The Saint Valentine's Day Massacre*. True or false?

. . . Answers

193. Wally Cox

194. The New York City blackout of November 9, 1965

195. *The Court Jester* and Danny Kaye

196. c

197. *A Fistful of Dollars*

198. Jack Palance

199. False (he plays Al Capone)

QUESTIONS

200) In *June Bride*, who plays the magazine writer that boss Bette Davis falls for while they do a story together about the title subject?

201) Glenda Jackson won an Oscar starring with Alan Bates and Oliver Reed in what adaptation of a D.H. Lawrence novel?

202) Who stars as the Thracian slave in *Spartacus*?

203) Who plays Gary Cooper's young deputy in *High Noon*?

204) Robert Young, a map-maker, Walter Brennan, his friend, and Spencer Tracy, the leader of Rogers' Rangers, battle Indians and the French in what film?

205) Who stars as the renegade fireman in the filmization of Ray Bradbury's *Fahrenheit 451*?

206) A cast of all-stars searches for a hidden treasure in *It's a Mad Mad Mad Mad World*. Where is it buried?

207) Who is John Wayne's love interest in *Operation Pacific*?

208) Richard Benjamin makes his debut wooing Ali McGraw in what movie?

209) In *Let's Make Love*, who plays the millionaire who goes all out to win Marilyn Monroe's affections?

. . . *Answers*

200. Robert Montgomery

201. *Women in Love*

202. Kirk Douglas

203. Lloyd Bridges

204. *Northwest Passage*

205. Oskar Werner

206. In a park under a big "W"

207. Patricia Neal

208. *Goodbye Columbus*

209. Yves Montand

QUESTIONS

210) What movie focuses on the sexual attitudes of friends Jack Nicholson and Art Garfunkel from college through middle-age?

211) Evel Knievel stars in the 1972 film *Evel Knievel*. True or false?

212) Who plays writer George Plimpton in *Paper Lion*?

213) What 1970 love story set in Northern Ireland has Sara Miles marrying schoolteacher Robert Mitchum?

214) In what 1971 film does retired judge George C. Scott think he's Sherlock Holmes? The psychiatrist (Joanne Woodward) who checks on him just happens to be named Dr. Watson.

215) Raymond St. Jacques and Godfrey Cambridge costar as cops in Harlem in what film directed by Ossie Davis?

216) Who plays Tevye in *Fiddler on the Roof*?

217) Jack Lemmon made his directorial debut in what film that stars Walter Matthau as an elderly man who lives with his son and daughter-in-law?

218) Joseph Bologna and Renee Taylor wrote and starred in what 1971 movie in which two screwballs meet and fall in love at an encounter group?

. . . *Answers*

210. *Carnal Knowledge*

211. False (George Hamilton)

212. Alan Alda

213. *Ryan's Daughter*

214. *They Might Be Giants*

215. *Cotton Comes to Harlem*

216. Topol

217. *Kotch*

218. *Made for Each Other*

219) Martin Sheen and Sissy Spacek play a young couple who go on a murder spree in what film?

220) Marsha Mason is a hooker with a black son and James Caan is the sailor who loves her in what film?

221) Richard Burton plays the priest in *The Exorcist*. True or false?

222) Who directed the 1973 film *Mean Streets*?

223) *Watership Down* is a German comedy about a U-boat with a leak. True or false?

224) Who won an Oscar for playing Dudley Moore's butler in *Arthur*?

225) Who played the female lead in *The Competition*?

226) Who is the male co-star with John Hurt in *The Elephant Man*?

227) *The Jazz Singer* was made in 1927, 1953 and 1980. Name the lead in each movie.

228) Catherine Deneuve hides her Jewish husband-director in their theater's basement during the Nazi occupation of Paris in what film?

229) What actor made his debut as a director in *Ordinary People*?

. . . Answers

219. *Badlands*

220. *Cinderella Liberty*

221. False (he's in *Exorcist II*)

222. Martin Scorsese

223. False (it's about rabbits)

224. John Gielgud

225. Amy Irving

226. Anthony Hopkins

227. Al Jolson, Danny Thomas and Neil Diamond

228. *The Last Metro*

229. Robert Redford

230) Robert DeNiro stars in *Raging Bull* as which boxer?

231) What film features the Band's final concert together in 1976 and includes appearances by Bob Dylan, Neil Young, Joni Mitchell and Eric Clapton?

232) What was Diane Keaton's profession in *Looking for Mr. Goodbar*?

233) Who directed *An Unmarried Woman*?

234) Who plays the policeman opposite Faye Dunaway in *Eyes of Laura Mars*?

235) Spencer Tracy plays a one-armed man in what 1954 movie?

236) What movie features Tony Curtis as the editor of a girlie magazine pursuing psychologist Natalie Wood?

237) In the 1949 film *The Third Man*, Joseph Cotton is searching for whom in post-World War II Vienna?

238) Who plays the lead role in *Joan of Arc*?

239) Paul Scofield won an Oscar for Best Actor, and the film Best Picture in 1966, in this story of the conflict between Sir Thomas More and Henry VIII. What is the film?

. . . *Answers*

230. Jake LaMotta

231. *The Last Waltz*

232. Schoolteacher

233. Paul Mazursky

234. Tommy Lee Jones

235. *Bad Day at Black Rock*

236. *Sex and the Single Girl*

237. Orson Welles (as Harry Lime)

238. Ingrid Bergman

239. *A Man for All Seasons*

240) What two actresses won Oscars for *Who's Afraid of Virginia Woolf?*

241) Conservative attorney Peter Sellers tries out hippie lifestyle in what movie?

242) American boxer John Wayne romances Irish beauty Maureen O'Hara in what John Ford film?

243) In *Five Easy Pieces*, Jack Nicholson makes a big fuss over what menu item?

244) She starred in the movie and the TV version of *Our Miss Brooks*.

245) In *Rabbit Test*, who plays the world's first pregnant man?

246) In *Making Love*, who discovers that her husband is having an affair with another man?

247) Who directed the 1982 film *One From the Heart*?

248) What actress invested in silicon implants in order to get the role of a Playboy centerfold in *Star 80*?

249) What Sidney Poitier movie introduced Lulu to America?

250) Muhammad Ali stars in a film of his own life. Name the film.

. . . Answers

240. Elizabeth Taylor and Sandy Dennis

241. *I Love You, Alice B. Toklas*

242. *The Quiet Man*

243. An egg salad sandwich

244. Eve Arden

245. Billy Crystal

246. Kate Jackson

247. Francis Ford Coppola

248. Mariel Hemingway

249. *To Sir, With Love*

250. *The Greatest*

251) What 1977 Oscar-winning documentary tells the story of striking Kentucky mine workers?

252) What actress plays the schizophrenic in *I Never Promised You a Rose Garden*?

253) Art Carney is a detective and Lily Tomlin a scatterbrained woman who tags along with him as he tries to solve the mystery of his partner's death in what film?

254) Who plays Dustin Hoffman's brother in *Marathon Man*?

255) What former *Rowan and Martin's Laugh-In* regular stars in *Get Christie Love*?

256) Glenda Jackson stars as the Mother Superior in what comedy involving a Watergate-type coverup in a convent?

257) What two actors teamed successfully in *48 hours*?

258) What former British star directed *Gandhi*?

259) He plays Jolly, Sally Field's deceased husband who comes back as a ghost to disrupt her upcoming marriage to Jeff Bridges in *Kiss Me Goodbye*. Who is he?

260) Marsha Mason's long-lost father, Jason Robards, returns to see her and her son in what Neil Simon story?

. . . Answers

251. *Harlan County, U.S.A.*

252. Kathleen Quinlan

253. *The Late Show*

254. Roy Scheider

255. Teresa Graves

256. *Nasty Habits*

257. Nick Nolte and Eddie Murphy

258. Richard Attenborough

259. James Caan

260. *Max Dugan Returns*

QUESTIONS

261) Sean Connery plays Robin Hood and Audrey Hepburn plays Maid Marian in *Robin and Marian*. Who plays Little John?

262) Who plays Carole Lombard in *Gable and Lombard*?

263) Who starred in and directed *The Adventures of Sherlock Holmes' Smarter Brother*?

264) What recent movie included in its cast of characters a one-legged tap dancer?

265) What 1975 Canadian film tells the story of the relationship between a boy and his grandfather in the Jewish ghetto in Montreal in 1924?

266) Who directed *Excalibur*?

267) Lauren Bacall is stalked by an overzealous admirer in what film?

268) Who directed Richard Pryor and Gene Wilder in *Stir Crazy*?

269) In *Claudine*, Diahann Carroll falls in love with a garbageman. Who plays the garbageman?

270) Her husband directed her in *The Effects of Gamma Rays on Man-in-the-Moon Marigolds*. Name him.

. . . Answers

261. Nicol Williamson

262. Jill Clayburgh

263. Gene Wilder

264. *Broadway Danny Rose*

265. *Lies My Father Told Me*

266. John Boorman

267. *The Fan*

268. Sidney Poitier

269. James Earl Jones

270. Paul Newman (His wife is Joanne Woodward.)

271) What 1973 film based on a best-seller tells the story of unique (at the time) co-ed college dormitories?

272) Who plays Brando's roomie in *Last Tango in Paris*?

273) What TV grandfather plays the mountain hermit in *Jeremiah Johnson*?

274) What actress stars opposite Sean Connery's Bond in *Diamonds Are Forever*?

275) Who stars as the English aristrocrat who is captured by the Indians in *A Man Called Horse*?

276) What athlete stars with Ann-Margret in *C.C. and Company*?

277) Who plays the American president in *Fail-Safe*?

278) Clifton Webb and Myrna Loy head the Gilbreth clan in what film?

279) Who stars in the 1932 film *Mata Hari*?
    a. Marlene Dietrich
    b. Greta Garbo
    c. Claudette Colbert
    d. Virginia Mayo

280) Ray Milland is a chemist who concocts a substance which causes baseballs to avoid bats in what movie?

. . . Answers

271. *The Harrad Experiment*

272. Maria Schneider

273. Will Geer

274. Jill St. John

275. Richard Harris

276. Joe Namath

277. Henry Fonda

278. *Cheaper by the Dozen*

279. b

280. *It Happens Every Spring*

281) In *The Seven Little Foys*, who plays the head Foy?

282) What real-life family is portrayed in *The Royal Family*?

283) Who plays Katherine Hepburn's incessantly potted brother in *Holiday*?

284) What 1975 Western starring Gene Hackman and James Coburn features a grueling six-hundred-mile horse race?

285) Carroll O'Connor and Ernest Borgnine become auxiliary cops to deal with the rising rate of crime in their neighborhood in what movie?

286) Who stars as Xaviera Hollander in *The Happy Hooker*?

287) "A Time for Us" was the theme of what 1968 film?

288) Who play the two sisters in *Whatever Happened to Baby Jane*?

289) Who did not appear in *The Wild Bunch*?
   a. Ben Johnson
   b. Warren Oates
   c. Jack Elam
   d. Strother Martin

. . . *Answers*

281. Bob Hope

282. The Barrymores

283. Lew Ayres

284. *Bite the Bullet*

285. *Law and Disorder*

286. Lynn Redgrave

287. *Romeo and Juliet*

288. Bette Davis and Joan Crawford

289. c

QUESTIONS

290) Dudley Moore sells his soul to devil Peter Cook in a comedy based on Faust. Name this 1967 movie.

291) Shirley MacLaine stars as a kind-hearted prostitute involved with a naive man who doesn't know what she does in what film?

292) Who is the leader of the group that is trying to break into the U.S. Mint in order to replace money that he accidently burned in *Who's Minding the Mint*?

293) Who plays the manager of a garish old New Orleans hotel trying to keep it from being bought by a national conglomerate in *Hotel*?

294) Steve McQueen and Richard Crenna star in what drama about an American gunboat in China during the 1920s?

295) Phil Silvers, Zero Mostel and Jack Gilford romp around ancient Rome in what 1966 comedy?

296) George C. Scott co-stars with what actress in the satire *The Hospital*?

297) Who played Boone in *Animal House* and then showed his versatility by playing a more or less straight role in *Local Hero*?

298) What career does Judy David pursue in the 1979 Autralian film *My Brilliant Career*?

. . . *Answers*

299) Dennis Christopher and pals are known collectively by what name in *Breaking Away*?

300) What director plays the UFO investigator in *Close Encounters of the Third Kind*?

301) What basketball star plays a pilot in *Airplane*?

302) Who plays the lead in *The Story of Louis Pasteur*?

303) In *House of Wax*, who plays Vincent Price's mute servant?

304) Identify the film and the speaker of the following line: "Now I'm going to take you in my arms and kiss you very long, and very hard."

305) Robert Redford stars as an aviator in what George Roy Hill film?

306) Who played the half-brothers in *The Vikings*?

307) In what film does a doctor change a man into a king cobra?

308) Jack Haley, Jr. directed both parts of *That's Entertainment*. True or false?

309) In *Fun With Dick and Jane*, who played Dick and Jane?

. . . Answers

299. Cutters

300. Francois Truffaut

301. Kareem Abdul-Jabbar

302. Paul Muni

303. Charles Bronson

304. *The Seven Year Itch* and Tom Ewell

305. *The Great Waldo Pepper*

306. Tony Curtis and Kirk Douglas

307. *Sssssss*

308. False (Gene Kelly directed Part II)

309. George Segal and Jane Fonda

QUESTIONS

310) In what film is Debbie Reynolds torn between her religious order and a recording career?

311) John Travolta won the Oscar for Best Supporting Actor for the 1978 film *Moment by Moment*. True or false?

312) Which actor stars in *The Love Bug*?
    a. Dean Jagger
    b. Dean Jones
    c. Dean Chance
    d. Tim Conway

313) Who plays Onionhead in the film of the same name?

314) Who sings the title song in the 1963 version of *Follow the Boys*?

315) Who plays the monster in the 1951 movie *The Thing (From Another World)*?

316) In what film does Edward G. Robinson play a doctor who joins a gang in order to study the inner workings of the criminal mind?

317) *The Man Who Knew Too Much* was produced in 1934 and again in 1956. Who directed each version?

. . . *Answers*

310. *The Singing Nun*

311. False

312. b

313. Andy Griffith

314. Connie Francis

315. James Arness

316. *The Amazing Dr. Clitterhouse*

317. Alfred Hitchcock

318) What movie included the following sketches: "Twit of the Year," "Joke Warfare," and "How to Protect Yourself From Being Attacked by Someone Wielding Fresh Fruit?

319) In how many films does Zeppo appear as the fourth Marx Brother?

320) What 1973 musical features the song "Day by Day"?

321) James Coburn invites six friends on board his yacht in the Riviera to discover which one murdered his wife in what film?

322) Who falls in love with Cybill Shepherd while on his honeymoon in *The Heartbreak Kid*?

323) What martial arts expert stars in *Lone Wolf McQuaid*?

324) What TV "hunk" stars opposite Bess Armstrong in *The High Road to China*?

325) What Louis Malle film follows the conversation that takes place between two friends during a repast?

326) What film tells the story of two women athletes who have a lesbian affair while competing for the Olympic team?

$\ldots$ Answers

318. *And Now for Something Completely Different*

319. Five

320. *Godspell*

321. *The Last of Sheila*

322. Charles Grodin

323. Chuck Norris

324. Tom Selleck

325. *My Dinner With Andre*

326. *Personal Best*

QUESTIONS

327) What city is the setting for *The Great Muppet Caper*?

328) In *Cool Hand Luke*, what is the name that George Kennedy gives to the beautiful woman who is tantalizing the men while she washes her car?

329) Clint Eastwood stars as the independent-minded cop in *Dirty Harry*. What is his character's last name?

330) There was a movie titled *Teenagers From Outer Space*. True or false?

331) Who played God in *Oh, God!*?

332) From which film is this quote: "Be happy in your work"?

333) Gregory Peck goes undercover to learn about anti-Semitism in this film that won the Oscar for Best Picture in 1947. Name the film.

334) Who did the score for the movie *High Noon*?

335) Who are the two protagonists in *Emperor of the North Pole*?

336) The original Three Stooges consisted of Moe Howard, Larry Fine and who else?

. . . *Answers*

327. London

328. Lucille

329. Callahan

330. True

331. George Burns

332. *The Bridge On the River Kwai*

333. *Gentleman's Agreement*

334. Dmitri Tiomkin

335. Lee Marvin and Ernest Borgnine

336. Curly Howard

337) Raquel Welch starred in which of these films?
   a. *Hannie Caulder*
   b. *The Three Musketeers*
   c. *Kansas City Bomber*
   d. *One Million Years B.C.*

338) Who plays Van Johnson's defense attorney in *The Caine Mutiny*?

339) George Romero directed what hard-to-swallow horror cult classic in 1968?

340) Who created *The Pink Panther*?

341) In which film do these songs appear: "Marian the Librarian," "Til' There Was You" and "The Sadder but Wiser Girl for Me"?

342) What disaster occurs in the 1958 British film *A Night to Remember*?

343) What was James Cagney's profession in *The Strawberry Blonde*?

344) This line is taken from what movie? "War is too important to be left to the politicians."

345) As a child, he had his own TV series, and later he starred in *Maya* and *Zebra in the Kitchen*. Who is he?

346) What 1975 movie is a spoof of beauty contests?

. . . *Answers*

337. All four

338. Jose Ferrer

339. *Night of the Living Dead*

340. Blake Edwards

341. *The Music Man*

342. The sinking of the *Titanic*

343. A dentist

344. *Patton*

345. Jay North

346. *Smile*

347) Henry Winkler plays a professional wrestler in what film?

348) John Belushi plays straight man to Dan Aykroyd in what 1981 film?

349) What 1975 film tells the story of a black youth who, after winning a basketball scholarship, is innocently shot by the police?

350) In *Funny Lady*, Fanny Brice (Barbra Streisand) marries James Caan. What character does Caan play?

351) Who plays detective Matt Helm in *The Ambushers*?

352) In *The Day of the Triffids*, what are Triffids?

353) George Burns, Art Carney and Lee Strasberg star as retirees who plan to rob a bank in what 1979 film?

354) In the film *Snoopy, Come Home*, why did Snoopy leave in the first place?

355) Ronald Reagan once starred in a film with the Bowery Boys. True or false?

356) Who plays the gourmet magazine publisher in *Who Is Killing the Great Chefs of Europe*?

. . . *Answers*

347. *The One and Only*

348. *Neighbors*

349. *Cornbread, Earl and Me*

350. Billy Rose

351. Dean Martin

352. Man-eating plants

353. *Going in Style*

354. To find a place without any "No Dogs Allowed" signs

355. True (*Hell's Kitchen*)

356. Robert Morley

357) Dana Andrews, investigating the alleged murder of Gene Tierney, sees her portrait and falls in love in what classic mystery?

358) What is the name of the movie that stars a near-sighted predator?

359) Straight cop Ryan O'Neal and homosexual cop John Hurt team up and pretend to be lovers in order to catch a murderer in what movie?

360) In John Cassavetes' *Gloria*, who stars as the former moll on the run from the mob?

361) Ingrid Bergman stars in Ingmar Bergman's film *Autumn Sonata*. True or false?

362) Bette Midler stars in *The Rose*, a film based on whose life?

363) One of the stars of *The China Syndrome* also produced the movie. Which star?

364) What TV teenager has a supporting role in *Cat Ballou*?

365) In *Harold and Maude*, he is a twenty-year-old who falls in love with a seventy-nine-year-old woman. Name these two actors.

. . . Answers

357. *Laura*

358. *Clarence, the Cross-Eyed Lion*

359. *Partners*

360. Gena Rowlands

361. True

362. Janis Joplin

363. Michael Douglas

364. Dwayne Hickman

365. Bud Cort and Ruth Gordon

366) Peter O'Toole plays the only British survivor when the Germans destroy his ship in what 1971 film?

367) Farley Granger plays Lot in the biblical saga *Sodom and Gomorrah*. True or false?

368) Gary Cooper portrays what baseball player in *Pride of the Yankees*?

369) In which of these films does Katherine Ross not co-star with Robert Redford?
   a. *Butch Cassidy and the Sundance Kid*
   b. *The Candidate*
   c. *Tell Them Willie Boy Is Here*

370) Which Astaire and Rogers film features the songs "The Continental" and "Night and Day"?

371) Peter MacNicol plays what character in *Sophie's Choice*?

372) Who is the voice of the mule in *Francis*?

373) What film features "the oldest established, permanent floating crap game in New York"?

374) Jackie Gleason plays Minnesota Fats in *The Hustler*. True or false?

375) The Rolling Stones filmed their 1981 tour. The movie's title is also one of their hit songs. What is it?

. . . Answers

366. *Murphy's War*

367. False (Stewart Granger)

368. Lou Gehrig

369. b

370. *The Gay Divorcee*

371. Stingo

372. Chill Wills

373. *Guys and Dolls*

374. True

375. *Let's Spend the Night Together*

376) What actor stars in *Cyrano de Bergerac*?

377) What film written by Dr. Seuss stars Hans Conried as a cruel piano teacher?

378) Who plays Dr. Watson to Basil Rathbone's Holmes?

379) What movie parody actually consisted of two separate features starring George C. Scott and Trish Van Devere?

380) In *The Great Escape*, who plays the Cooler King?

381) Who plays James Dean's father in *Rebel Without a Cause*?

382) The soul of Eddie "Rochester" Anderson is fought over by the forces of good and evil in what film?

383) Two six-inch girls befriend a giant caterpillar. The girls are kidnapped by a circus owner, and the monster destroys most of Tokyo while rescuing them. Name this film?

384) *Ice Station Zebra* has an all-male cast. True or false?

385) What comedy team starred in the 1969 film *The Maltese Bippy*?

. . . *Answers*

376. Jose Ferrer

377. *The 5000 Fingers of Dr. T*

378. Nigel Bruce

379. *Movie Movie*

380. Steve McQueen

381. Jim Backus

382. *Cabin in the Sky*

383. *Mothra*

384. True

385. Dan Rowan and Dick Martin

QUESTIONS

386) In *The Great Santini*, Robert Duvall is a fighter pilot in what branch of the service?

387) Who plays Dustin Hoffman's coquettish wife in *Straw Dogs*?

388) William Powell is a wealthy Bostonian who conceals his background and works as a butler in what classic comedy?

389) Who plays the White Knight in the 1933 version of *Alice in Wonderland*?

390) What are the tiny workers called in *Willie Wonka and the Chocolate Factory*?

391) The 1978 film *Heaven Can Wait* is a remake of what movie?

392) What film features a house full of weirdos from the planet Transylvania?

393) Who abducts Samantha Eggar in *The Collector*?

394) Peter Sellers falls for what actress in *There's a Girl in My Soup*?

395) In the movie *Nashville*, who won an Oscar for the song "I'm Easy"?

396) What city was the setting for *A Raisin in the Sun*?

. . . Answers

386. The Marines

387. Susan George

388. *My Man Godfrey*

389. Gary Cooper

390. Oompa-Loompas

391. *Here Comes Mr. Jordan*

392. *The Rocky Horror Picture Show*

393. Terrence Stamp

394. Goldie Hawn

395. Keith Carradine

396. Chicago

397) Who is the star of the 1963 film *The Stripper*?

398) Which one of these performers did *not* appear in a Three Stooges short?
    a. Dan Blocker
    b. Lucille Ball
    c. Alan Hale
    d. Walter Brennan

399) Maggie Smith won an Oscar for her portrayal of an Edinburgh schoolteacher in what movie?

400) Who directed Dick Van Dyke in *The Comic*?

401) *The Sting* was the second film to feature Paul Newman with Robert Redford. True or false?

402) *High Society* was a musical remake of what film?

403) What is hijacked in *The Taking of Pelham One Two Three*?

404) Name the film from the following quote: "C'mon, Norman. They're openin' up the bah."

405) Paul Muni plays an innocent man sent to jail in what 1932 film?

406) What was Cary Grant's criminal nickname in *To Catch a Thief*?

. . . *Answers*

397. Joanne Woodward

398. c

399. *The Prime of Miss Jean Brodie*

400. Carl Reiner

401. True

402. *The Philadelphia Story*

403. A New York City subway train

404. *The Russians Are Coming, the Russians Are Coming*

405. *I Am a Fugitive From a Chain Gang*

406. The Cat

407) Tony Curtis plays the title role in *Lepke*, the head gangster of what organization?

408) Vivien Leigh is featured in *Psycho*. True or false?

409) Audrey Hepburn is a blind girl and Alan Arkin a psychopath in what thriller?

410) What character does Percy Gilbride play in a series of movies in the late forties and early fifties?

411) Who plays the female lead in Hitchcock's *Rebecca*?

412) What Pulitzer Prize-winning cartoonist has a supporting role in the 1951 version of *The Red Badge of Courage*?

413) Who is W.C. Fields' main antagonist in *Tillie and Gus*?

414) Spencer Tracy is an efficiency expert clashing with TV executive Katherine Hepburn in what film?

415) In *Blithe Spirit*, newlywed Rex Harrison is haunted by the ghost of his first wife. Who plays his second wife?

416) Scientist Lew Ayres finds his behavior is being controlled by a brain that he has preserved in what 1953 film?

...Answers

407. Murder, Inc.

408. False (Janet Leigh)

409. *Wait Until Dark*

410. Pa Kettle

411. Joan Fontaine

412. Bill Mauldin

413. Baby LeRoy

414. *Desk Set*

415. Constance Cummings

416. *Donovan's Brain*

417) Ronald Colman is an actor who is unable to distinguish between his real life and his role of Othello in what melodrama?

418) What former professional baseball and basketball player, and TV cowboy, stars in the 1962 film *Geronimo*?

419) Who stars as the tap-dancing magician in the 1973 comedy *Get to Know Your Rabbit*?

420) Who plays the head of the household in *Munster, Go Home*?

421) Who is Dracula in Werner Herzog's *Nosferatu*?

422) What actor is The Scarlet Pimpernel in the 1934 production?
   a. Noel Coward
   b. Douglas Fairbanks, Jr.
   c. Leslie Howard
   d. Franchot Tone

423) John Wayne, Dean Martin, Earl Holliman and Michael Anderson return to their home town to avenge their mother's death in what western?

424) Ralph Richardson stars in a documentary-style film about the early days of jet planes. Name the film.

. . . *Answers*

417. *A Double Life*

418. Chuck Connors

419. Tommy Smothers

420. Fred Gwynne

421. Klaus Kinski

422. c

423. *The Sons of Katie Elder*

424. *Breaking the Sound Barrier*

425) Reporter James Stewart sets out to clear an innocent man convicted of murder eleven years earlier in what 1948 film?

426) Who plays the gangster Hyman Roth in *The Godfather, Part II*?

427) What Woody Allen film stars an Oriental spy named Phil Moscowitz?

428) Robby Benson is a hot-shot basketball player in what film?

429) Herman's Hermits are featured in what 1966 film that has the same name as one of their hit songs?

430) Who is the lead in the film *W.C. Fields and Me*?

431) Who inherits a cat house in *The Cheyenne Social Club*?

432) Nathaniel West's novel of sordid and shallow Hollywood in the 1930s is depicted in what 1975 film starring Karen Black and Donald Sutherland?

433) What boxer, renowned for busting Muhammad Ali's jaw, is the stud slave in *Mandingo*?

434) Richard Burton and Clint Eastwood lead a group of soldiers trying to free an American officer held in a German mountain castle in what 1969 adventure?

. . . Answers

425. *Call Northside 777*

426. Lee Strasberg

427. *What's Up, Tiger Lily?*

428. *One on One*

429. *Hold On!*

430. Rod Steiger

431. James Stewart

432. *The Day of the Locust*

433. Ken Norton

434. *Where Eagles Dare*

435) What was Robert Morse initially employed as in *How to Succeed in Business Without Really Trying*?

436) What is the name of the kiddie-show host in *A Thousand Clowns*?

437) What is Al Pacino in *The Panic in Needle Park*?

438) Who plays the minister leading an entire town to quit smoking in *Cold Turkey*?

439) In *Everything You Always Wanted to Know About Sex (But Were Afraid to Ask)*, who plays the crazed sex therapist who was kicked out of Masters and Johnson's for his unorthodox experiments?

440) Sheriff Kirk Douglas must shoot it out with old friend Anthony Quinn in order to get Quinn's son who has murdered Kirk's wife in what western?

441) Frank Sinatra is a playboy adulated by his kid brother, and Lee J. Cobb is his concerned father in what Neil Simon filmization?

442) Charlton Heston, Ava Gardner and David Niven star in *55 Days in Peking*. This movie tells the story of what historical event?

443) What 1941 drama with Walter Pidgeon and Maureen O'Hara depicts the life of Welsh coal miners?

. . . *Answers*

435. A window washer

436. Chuckles the Chipmunk

437. A heroin addict

438. Dick Van Dyke

439. John Carradine

440. *Last Train From Gun Hill*

441. *Come Blow Your Horn*

442. The Boxer Rebellion

443. *How Green Was My Valley*

444) What was the lioness' name in *Born Free*?

445) What part does Humphrey Bogart play in his last feature film *The Harder They Fall*?
    a. Boxer
    b. Manager
    c. Press Agent
    d. Cut man
    e. Bookie

446) George Tobias, before becoming Gary Cooper's pal in *Sergeant York*, worked on the N.Y.C. subway stuffing people into streetcars. His name in this movie was derived from his job. What was his name?

447) In *Double Indemnity*, who talks Fred MacMurray into committing a murder?

448) Bette Davis is dying in *Dark Victory*. Who plays her surgeon-husband?

449) Cary Grant, a professor married to Ginger Rogers, discovers a "mental" youth serum in what Howard Hawks comedy?

450) Who stars as the leader of an expedition to Tibet in *The Mole People*?

451) What musical has as its plot Judy Garland replacing Ann Miller as Fred Astaire's dancing partner?

. . . *Answers*

444. Elsa

445. c

446. Pusher

447. Barbara Stanwyck

448. George Brent

449. *Monkey Business*

450. John Agar

451. *Easter Parade*

452) Robert Blake plays a short motorcycle cop in what film?

453) What character does Joe Flynn portray in the movie *McHale's Navy*?

454) Who stars as the paranoid prisoner in *Riot in Cell Block 11*?

455) *Operation Bikini*, in 1963, is a war movie starring Frankie Avalon. True or false?

456) What is the only film which stars both Mae West and W.C. Fields?

457) Who stars opposite John Lund as an Iowa congresswoman visiting Berlin in the post-World War II satire *A Foreign Affair*?

458) Edward G. Robinson plays *Little Caesar*. What is Caesar's full name?

459) What Frederick Wiseman documentary shows life on the inside of a Massachusetts mental hospital?

460) In what musical does Doris Day play the head of a grievance committee in a factory?

461) What "big mouth" plays the baseball pitcher in Ring Lardner's story *Alibi Ike*?

... *Answers*

452. *Electra Glide in Blue*

453. Captain Wallace Binghamton

454. Neville Brand

455. True

456. *My Little Chickadee*

457. Jean Arthur

458. Caesar Enrico Bandella

459. *Titicut Follies*

460. *The Pajama Game*

461. Joe E. Brown

462) Who is Woody Allen's co-star in *Take the Money and Run*?

    a. Janet Margolin
    b. Diane Keaton
    c. Louise Lasser
    d. Mia Farrow

463) What Rodgers and Hammerstein musical stars Gordon McRae, Shirley Jones and Gloria Grahame?

464) In *Popeye*, who play Popeye and Olive Oyl?

465) Who directed the 1931 German film *M*?

466) Shirley Booth won an Oscar as the slovenly wife of alcoholic Burt Lancaster in what film?

467) Who plays the lead in the 1933 version of *The Invisible Man*?

468) What film stars Brad Davis in the true story of an American in Turkey who is sent to prison for smuggling hashish?

469) Which of the following monsters did Godzilla not duke it out with?

    a. the Smog Monster
    b. the Cosmic Monster
    c. the Fire Monster
    d. the Space Monster

. . . Answers

462. a

463. *Oklahoma!*

464. Robin Williams and Shelley Duval

465. Fritz Lang

466. *Come Back, Little Sheba*

467. Claude Rains

468. Midnight Express

469. d

QUESTIONS

470) In *It Happened One Night*, who sings "Young people in love very seldom get hungry"?

471) Who directed Elliot Gould in *The Long Goodbye*?

472) Better known as a writer extraordinaire of Broadway comedies, he directed the 1947 film *The Senator Was Indiscreet*. Who is he?

473) Who plays the well-preserved monster in the 1932 version of *The Mummy*?

474) Albert Brooks directs and stars in a spoof about the filming of a typical American family. Name the film.

475) What film, starring Anthony Quinn, caused a huge uproar in the Arab world when it was released in 1977?

476) The cast includes Clint Eastwood, George Kennedy and Jack Cassidy, but the real star is a Swiss mountain peak in what movie?

477) Peter Davis' documentary *Hearts and Minds* won an Oscar in 1975. It death with a controversial subject at the time. What was the subject?

478) Who plays the detective searching for a mass murderer in *The List of Adrian Messenger*?

. . . *Answers*

470. Alan Hale

471. Robert Altman

472. George S. Kaufman

473. Boris Karloff

474. *Real Life*

475. *Mohammad, Messenger of God*

476. *The Eiger Sanction*

477. Vietnam

478. George C. Scott

QUESTIONS

479) In 1963, the first James Bond film appeared. What was it?

480) Who plays the part of Pegeen in the 1962 Irish production of *Playboy of the Western World*?

481) Sidney Poitier won an Oscar as a handyman who encounters some nuns fleeing from East Germany and helps them build a chapel in what movie?

482) What Disney movie features a 250-mile trek across Canada by Muffey, Rink and Syn Cat?

483) Who stars as the reform school delinquent in the British film *The Loneliness of the Long Distance Runner*?

484) What Eugene O'Neill adaptation stars Katherine Hepburn as a dope addict, Ralph Richardson as her pompous husband, Jason Robards as their alcoholic son and Dean Stockwell as his TB-ridden brother?

485) Who plays Captain Bligh to Brando's Fletcher Christian?

486) Who plays Shoeless Joe Hardy in *Damn Yankees*?

487) David Niven, Gregory Peck and Anthony Quinn star in what film about Allied commandos trying to destroy a German stronghold?

. . . *Answers*

488) Who plays the black trumpeter struggling to make it big in the jazz world in *A Man called Adam*?

489) Who plays the convict who goes on to become a musical star in *Jailhouse Rock*?

490) In the 1978 film *Gray Lady Down*, a rescue is mounted to save what?
    a. an old woman
    b. valuable goose feathers
    c. a submarine
    d. a destroyer

491) Clark Gable and Spencer Tracy try out new aircraft and Myrna Loy provides the love interest in what 1938 movie?

492) Who stars in the role of *Tennessee Johnson*?

493) Dick Shawn tries to make the most of being assigned to a remote Far East island after World War II, so he builds a sumptuous hotel with army supplies in what film?

494) What comedy team stars in *Pardon My Sarong*?

495) What musical, starring Gene Kelly and Frank Sinatra, is about three sailors on leave in New York City?

. . . *Answers*

488. Sammy Davis, Jr.

489. Elvis Presley

490. c

491. *Test Pilot*

492. Van Heflin

493. *Wake Me When It's Over*

494. Abbott and Costello

495. *On the Town*

496) Samantha Eggar mistakenly agrees to share her apartment with Cary Grant and Jim Hutton during the Tokyo Olympics in what movie?

497) *Thunder Bay,* starring James Stewart and Joanne Dru, tells of the conflict between oil workers and fishermen. What is the main catch of the fishermen?

498) Brian Bedford and James Farentino are roommates and Julie Somers is the object of their affection in what movie?

499) Kim Novak is suspected of murdering her husband and tenant Jack Lemmon gets involved in finding out if she did in what movie?

500) Tyrone Power stars as a famous bandleader-pianist in what movie?

501) In what two movies does Clint Eastwood sing?

502) Who stars as the narcotics cop in New York in *The Prince of the City*?

503) Who plays the American reporter who greets Martin Sheen in the jungle near the end of *Apocalypse Now*?

504) Diane Keaton and Albert Finney star as a couple whose marriage is disintegrating in what 1982 film?

. . . *Answers*

496. *Walk, Don't Run*

497. Shrimp

498. *The Pad (and How to Use It)*

499. *The Notorious Landlady*

500. *The Eddie Duchin Story*

501. *Paint Your Wagon* and *Honkytonk Man*

502. Treat Williams

503. Dennis Hopper

504. *Shoot the Moon*

QUESTIONS

505) Tatum O'Neal and Kristy McNichol have a race to see who can lose her virginity first in what movie?

506) In *Rich and Famous*, two women remain best friends through various ups and downs. What actresses play these pals?

507) What movie, starring Burt Lancaster, Kirk Douglas and Frederic March, tells the story of the military trying to gain control of the American government?

508) Who plays Robin Hood in *Time Bandits*?

509) Who plays Tony Curtis' wife in *Houdini*?

510) Who stars as the lead in *The Flower Drum Song*?

511) What actor plays Julie Andrews' gay friend in *Victor/Victoria*?

512) Gene Roddenberry directed *Star Trek — The Movie*. True or false?

513) James Cagney came out of retirement to star as a police commissioner in what film?

514) George Segal stars as an American POW in the Pacific in what 1965 film?

. . . *Answers*

505. *Little Darlings*

506. Candice Bergen and Jacqueline Bisset

507. *Seven Days in May*

508. John Cleese

509. Janet Leigh

510. Nancy Kwan

511. Robert Preston

512. False (Robert Wise)

513. *Ragtime*

514. *King Rat*

515) Errol Flynn and Olivia De Havilland do not appear together in which film?
  a. *Captain Blood*
  b. *Charge of the Light Brigade*
  c. *The Adventures of Robin Hood*
  d. *Gentleman Jim*
  e. *Dodge City*

516) Who is Daddy Warbucks in the film *Annie*?

517) Robert Mitchum plays a small-time Boston hood in a movie based on a novel by George V. Higgins. Name the movie.

518) Jamie Lee Curtis does not star in which of these films?
  a. *Halloween*
  b. *Friday the 13th*
  c. *Prom Night*

519) Nastassia Kinski plays a woman seduced in what Roman Polanski film?

520) Who plays Bill Murray's sergeant in *Stripes*?

521) Paul Newman is implicated in a labor leader's disappearance and uses reporter Sally Field to clear his name in what movie?

522) What movie stars Gary Cooper and Dorothy McGuire as Quakers during the Civil War?

. . . *Answers*

515. d

516. Albert Finney

517. *The Friends of Eddie Coyle*

518. b

519. *Tess*

520. Warren Oates

521. *Absence of Malice*

522. *Friendly Persuasion*

523) In *The Deer Hunter*, what actor stays behind in Vietnam and becomes a pro Russian roulette player?

524) Who directed *The Lord of the Rings*?

525) Alan Alda plays a liberal senator in what film?

526) Who won the Oscar for Best Supporting Actor for playing an aging, influential businessman in *Being There*?

527) Who spends most of *Caddyshack* trying to eliminate a pesky gopher from a golf course?

528) By what name did Steve Martin call his dog in *The Jerk*?

529) Diana Ross plays a famous fashion designer who learns that success can be lonely in what movie?

530) In John Wayne's last movie, he plays an aging gunfighter who is dying of cancer. Name the 1976 film.

531) Glenn Ford plays a New York City schoolteacher trying to reach delinquent students in what film?

532) In *Close Encounters of the Third Kind*, Richard Dreyfuss and others are compelled to go to a specific site. Name this landmark.

. . . *Answers*

523. Christopher Walken

524. Ralph Bakshi

525. *The Seduction of Joe Tynan*

526. Melvyn Douglas

527. Bill Murray

528. Shithead

529. *Mahogany*

530. *The Shootist*

531. *The Blackboard Jungle*

532. Devil's Mountain

QUESTIONS

533) Who plays the Jackie Onassis character in *The Greek Tycoon*?

534) What actor narrates *Marilyn*, a semi-documentary look at Marilyn Monroe?

535) What was the name of the character played by Robert DeNiro in *Taxi Driver*?

536) What war is the setting for *Pork Chop Hill*?

537) Who plays the ex-gunfighter in *Shane*?

538) Lee Grant won an Oscar for Best Actress for her part in *Shampoo*. True or false?

539) Joseph Bologna's character is modeled after what TV comedian in *My Favorite Year*?

540) *King Kong* had a thing for Fay Wray in the 1933 version. Who is the object of the ape's lust in 1976?

541) Who is Dustin Hoffman's roommate in *Tootsie*?

542) Who won an Oscar for Best Supporting Actor for *An Officer and a Gentleman*?

543) Who plays Derek Flint in the James Bond spoof *Our Man Flint*?

. . . Answers

533. Jacqueline Bisset

534. Rock Hudson

535. Travis Bickle

536. The Korean War

537. Alan Ladd

538. False (She won Best Supporting Actress)

539. Sid Caesar

540. Jessica Lange

541. Bill Murray

542. Louis Gossett, Jr.

543. James Coburn

544) Robert Mitchum and Deborah Kerr are Australian sheepherders in what 1960 movie?

545) Who stars as a young pianist getting involved with a satanic cult in *The Mephisto Waltz*?

546) Lillian Hellman is portrayed by Jane Fonda in what 1977 film?

547) Bob Hope, Bing Crosby and Dorothy Lamour never made one of the following *Road to . . .* movies. Which one?
   a. *Manila*
   b. *Morocco*
   c. *Singapore*
   d. *Zanzibar*

548) Who plays the president in *The First Family*?

549) Lloyd Nolan and William Bendix star in what action-packed World War II Pacific adventure?

550) The Beatles film *A Hard Day's Night* is animated. True or false?

551) Who plays the adolescent who falls in love with married Jennifer O'Neill in *Summer of '42*?

552) Who is Godfrey Cambridge's wife in *The Watermelon Man*?

. . . *Answers*

544. *The Sundowners*

545. Alan Alda

546. *Julia*

547. a

548. Bob Newhart

549. *Guadalcanal Diary*

550. False

551. Gary Grimes

552. Estelle Parsons

553) What film depicts the true story of three Australians brought to trial for their part in a massacre during the Boer War?

554) Maurice Chevalier sings "Thank Heaven, for Little Girls" in what movie?

555) James Cagney plays a reporter who is framed and sent to prison in what film?

556) Who stars as the black private-eye in *Shaft*?

557) *Rock 'n' Roll High School* features the music of what group?

558) Who plays Burt Reynolds' best friend and mechanic in *Stroker Ace*?

559) Who wants dumpy-looking Lynn Redgrave for his mistress in *Georgy Girl*?

560) In *The Birds*, who plays Rod Taylor's present girlfriend and former girlfriend?

561) Who plays the embittered agent in *The Spy Who Came in From the Cold*?

562) How is *The Blob* finally disposed of?

563) In *The Verdict*, who plays the woman who gains the trust of Paul Newman, only to turn on him?

. . . *Answers*

553. *Breaker Morant*

554. *Gigi*

555. *Each Dawn I Die*

556. Richard Roundtree

557. The Ramones

558. Jim Nabors

559. James Mason

560. Tippi Hedren and Suzanne Pleshette

561. Richard Burton

562. It is frozen and airlifted out of town by helicopter

563. Charlotte Rampling

564) Genevieve Bujold is Anne Boleyn and Richard Burton King Henry VIII in what 1964 film?

565) What 1971 film starring Bruce Davison and Ernest Borgnine tells the story of a boy and his rats?

566) Who plays Patty McCormack's mother in *The Bad Seed*?

567) Jason Robards is a prospector and Stella Stevens a prostitute who takes up with him in what Peckinpah film?

568) The movie *Going Ape* with George Segal and Ruth Gordon ws first released under what title?

569) Who stars as Buford Pusser's wife in *Walking Tall*?

570) Two children are stranded in the Australian outback and make it across the desert with the help of an aborigine in what film?

571) What William Friedkin film starring Cliff Gorman deals frankly with homosexuality?

572) Everything goes wrong for Sandy Dennis and Jack Lemmon on a visit to New York City in what Neil Simon adaptation?

. . . *Answers*

564. *Anne of a Thousand Days*

565. *Willard*

566. Nancy Kelly

567. *The Ballad of Cable Hogue*

568. *Where's Poppa?*

569. Elizabeth Hartman

570. *Walkabout*

571. *The Boys in the Band*

572. *The Out of Towners*

573) Rod Steiger stars as a store-owner in Harlem who has haunting memories of Nazi prison camps in what 1965 film?

574) Who is Pookie Adams in *The Sterile Cuckoo*?

575) In the sci-fi movie *Them!* what odor was a dead give-away that the monsters were near?

576) In what film did Sydney Greenstreet make his move debut?

577) Clint Eastwood helps nun Shirley MacLaine cross the Mexican desert in what 1970 western?

578) Who plays the race car driver in *Viva Las Vegas*?

579) What former child star plays the female lead opposite Phil Silvers in *Top Banana*?

580) In Hitchcock's *Topaz*, who plays the American official trying to ferret out Russia's involvement in Cuba?

581) Natalie Wood and Robert Culp introduce Dyan Cannon and Elliot Gould to a different lifestyle in what movie?

582) Who plays General Omar Bradley in *Patton*?

. . . Answers

573. *The Pawnbroker*

574. Liza Minnelli

575. Formic acid

576. *The Maltese Falcon*

577. *Two Mules for Sister Sara*

578. Elvis Presley

579. Rose Marie

580. John Forsythe

581. *Bob & Carol & Ted & Alice*

582. Karl Malden

583) In *The Secret of Santa Vittoria*, starring Anthony Quinn, an Italian town succeeds in hiding something from the Germans at the end of World War II. What did they hide?

584) What is the sequel to *In the Heat of the Night*?

585) What Fred Astaire-Ginger Rogers film features the songs "Pick Yourself Up" and "A Fine Romance"?

586) Who are the vaudeville couple in the 1947 musical *Mother Wore Tights*?

587) Henry Fonda tries to persuade his fellow jurors to reconsider their verdict in what film?

588) In what movie does James Cagney play a gangster with a mother fetish?

589) Connie Stevens is the original Gidget. True or false?

590) Who schemes to extricate himself from his marriage in *Divorce — Italian Style*?

591) Who play the two kidnappers of Stockard Channing in *The Fortune*?

592) James Stewart portrays a baseball player who loses a leg in what film?

. . . *Answers*

583. One million bottles of wine

584. *They Call Me Mr. Tibbs*

585. *Swing Time*

586. Betty Grable and Dan Dailey

587. *12 Angry Men*

588. *White Heat*

589. False (Sandra Dee)

590. Marcello Mastroianni

591. Jack Nicholson and Warren Beatty

592. *The Stratton Story*

QUESTIONS

593) Jean Arthur is Calamity Jane and Gary Cooper Wild Bill Hickok in what Cecil B. DeMille film?

594) Irwin Allen's first disaster film was the 1969 *Krakatoa, East of Java*. True or false?

595) What comedy starring Suzanne Pleshette tells the story of a bunch of travellers touring Europe and seeing seven countries in eighteen days?

596) Who won an Oscar for Best Supporting Actress for *Murder on the Orient Express*?
   a. Ingrid Bergman
   b. Lauren Bacall
   c. Vanessa Redgrave
   d. Rachel Roberts

597) Michael Moriarty is a cop who accidently kills undercover officer Susan Blakely and a department coverup ensues in what film?

598) Elizabeth Taylor and Peter Finch work a tea plantation on Ceylon in what film?

599) Dick Van Dyke stars in what musical about a flying car?

600) Who never played Quasimodo in *The Hunchback of Notre Dame*?
   a. Peter Cushing   c. Charles Laughton
   b. Anthony Quinn   d. Lon Chaney

. . . _Answers_

593. *The Plainsman*

594. False

595. *If It's Tuesday, This Must Be Belgium*

596. a

597. *Report to the Commissioner*

598. *Elephant Walk*

599. *Chitty Chitty Bang Bang*

600. a

601) What 1967 Swedish film about a woman sociologist caused an uproar because of the strong sexual content?

602) Lucille Ball, mother of eight, marries Henry Fonda, father of ten, in what 1968 comedy?

603) *Gone With the Wind* was released in 1968 for the first time with stereophonic sound and completely re-colored. True or false?

604) Julie Christie is the beautiful girl who dazzles Alan Bates, Peter Finch and Terrence Stamp in what film of a Thomas Hardy novel?

605) *Valley of the Dolls* depicts three women trying to make it in show business. Two of the women are Patty Duke and Barbara Parkins. Name the third.

606) In *The Incredible Mr. Limpet*, what does Don Knotts become?

607) John Wayne and Red Buttons are big-game hunters in Africa in what movie?

608) Burt Lancaster gets involved in selling stolen heroin in what 1981 film?

609) Lana Turner and Lloyd Nolan star in what 1957 film about the shady secrets of a New England town?

. . . Answers

601. *I Am Curious (Yellow)*

602. *Your, Mine and Ours*

603. True

604. *Far From the Madding Crowd*

605. Sharon Tate

606. A dolphin

607. *Hatari*

608. *Atlantic City*

609. *Peyton Place*

610) Steve McQueen is an aging rodeo star who goes home for one last contest in what movie?

611) Montgomery Clift must choose between rich and alluring Liz Taylor and drab Shelley Winters in what 1951 remake of Theodore Dreiser's *An American Tragedy*?

612) Who plays the title role in *Thoroughly Modern Millie*?

613) James Mason played Field Marshal Rommel in both *The Desert Fox* and *The Desert Rats*. True or false?

614) What was the original title of the Marx Brothers movie *Duck Soup*?

615) In the movie *Batman*, Adam West and Burt Ward are threatened by four of their arch enemies. Name all four.

616) James Stewart plays what character in *Harvey*?

617) Who does James Cagney portray in *Man of a Thousand Faces*?

618) What TV clown appears in the prologue of *Those Magnificent Men in Their Flying Machines* and gives a dissertation on the history of flying?

619) Who discovered Cary Grant?

620) Who plays John Adams in *1776*?

. . . *Answers*

610. *Junior Bonner*

611. *A Place in the Sun*

612. Julie Andrews

613. True

614. *Cracked Ice*

615. The Joker, the Riddler, the Penguin and the Catwoman

616. Elwood P. Dowd

617. Lon Chaney

618. Red Skelton

619. Mae West

620. William Daniels

621) Who portrays Al Capone in the 1932 *Scarface*?

622) What married couple stars in Dylan Thomas' *Under Milkwood*?

623) Bing Crosby won an Oscar for Best Actor in 1944 for *Going My Way*. True or false?

624) What songwriting team composed the music to *The Sound of Music*?

625) This 1949 movie won Oscars for its leading man and for its adaptation of Robert Penn Warren's novel about the rise and fall of a Huey Long-type politician. Name the actor and the film.

626) Which of the following actresses has not won two Best Actress Oscars?
    a. Luise Rainer
    b. Joan Crawford
    c. Ingrid Bergman
    d. Vivien Leigh
    e. Olivia De Havilland

627) The boy who played *Tom Sawyer* in 1973 also starred in a TV series with Brian Keith and Sebastian Cabot. Name him.

628) What 1971 film tells of the romance of museum curator Gena Rowlands and parking lot attendant Seymour Cassel?

. . . Answers

621. Paul Muni

622. Elizabeth Taylor and Richard Burton

623. True

624. Rodgers and Hammerstein

625. Broderick Crawford and *All the King's Men*

626. b

627. Johnny Whitaker

628. *Minnie and Moscowitz*

629) Who plays Bogart in *Play It Again, Sam*?

630) Jack Lemmon and Barbara Harris star in the comedy *The War Between Men and Women*. It is based on whose writings and cartoons?

631) What was the name of Harvey Korman's character in *Blazing Saddles*?

632) What film starring David Wayne is about a group of scientists racing against time to isolate a deadly virus?

633) *The New Centurions*, starring George C. Scott and Stacy Keach, is based on whose novel?

634) Michael Sacks plays Billy Pilgrim in what 1972 Vonnegut filmization?

635) In what movie does Santa Claus go on trial to prove he is for real?

636) In *The Paper Chase*, who stars as a first-year law student?

637) What is the name of the sequel to *Fritz the Cat*?

638) In *Mr. Roberts*, Jack Lemmon plays Ensign Pulver. What were his official duties on the ship?

639) In what Henry Fonda saga is an innocent man the victim of a lynch mob?

. . . *Answers*

629. Jerry Lacy

630. James Thurber

631. Hedy Lamarr

632. *The Andromeda Strain*

633. Joseph Wambaugh

634. *Slaughterhouse Five*

635. *Miracle on 34th Street*

636. Timothy Bottoms

637. *The Nine Lives of Fritz the Cat*

638. Laundry and Morale Officer

639. *The Ox-Bow Incident*

640) Who directs and stars in both *Kon-Tiki* and *The Ra Expeditions*?

641) Who are the two co-stars of *The Way We Were*?

642) What kind of a dog did Al Pacino own in *Serpico*?

643) Who plays Joanne Woodward's husband in *Summer Wishes, Winter Dreams*?

644) What was the sequel to *Westworld*?

645) George Segal becomes increasingly violent when a computer that controls his behavior goes amiss in what 1974 film?

646) Who stars opposite Barbra Streisand in the remake of *A Star Is Born*?

647) What 1977 film stars Michael Caine and Donald Sutherland and revolves around a Nazi plot to kidnap Winston Churchill?

648) Jack Lemmon lends boss Fred MacMurray the key to his flat for some "after hours" work in what Oscar-winning movie?

649) Boris Karloff narrates and stars in what 1964 horror trilogy?

. . . Answers

640. Thor Heyerdahl

641. Barbra Streisand and Robert Redford

642. A Saint Bernard

643. Martin Balsam

644. *Futureworld*

645. *The Terminal Man*

646. Kris Kristofferson

647. *The Eagle Has Landed*

648. *The Apartment*

649. *Black Sabbath*

650) Who does *Zelig* not appear with in news clips?
 a. Babe Ruth
 b. Adolf Hitler
 c. Charles Chaplin
 d. Charles Lindbergh

651) In *Twilight Zone — The Movie*, who plays the terrified airline passenger who spots a gremlin tampering with the plane's engine?

652) In *Escape from Alcatraz*, the prisoner — Clint Eastwood — was never found. True or false?

653) Who plays Lex Luthor in *Superman*?

654) Jim Henson directed *The Muppet Movie*. True or false?

655) *The Big Red One*, starring Lee Marvin, was supposed to be based on the experiences of its director. Name the director.

656) In *Kramer vs. Kramer*, the custody of a child is fought over. Who plays the child?

657) Gary Cooper plays a hobo who threatens suicide to protest world conditions in *Meet John Doe*. Who plays the newspaper reporter who falls in love with him?

. . . *Answers*

650. d

651. John Lithgow

652. True

653. Gene Hackman

654. False (James Frawley)

655. Sam Fuller

656. Justin Henry

657. Barbara Stanwyck

658) Richard Pryor, Harvey Keitel and Yaphet Kotto are auto workers who discover corruption in their union in what 1978 movie?

659) Keith Carradine and Harvey Keitel have an ongoing feud during the Napoleonic era in what film?

660) Marilyn Monroe plays a mediocre singer pursued by cowboy Don Murray in what film?

661) What western features the Keach, the Carradine and the Quaid brothers?

662) Mel Brooks does not appear in which of these films?
   a. *The Twelve Chairs*
   b. *Blazing Saddles*
   c. *The Producers*
   d. *High Anxiety*

663) Who plays Hildy Johnson in the 1940 screwball comedy *His Girl Friday*?

664) *The Jungle Book* is Rudyard Kipling's tale of a boy raised by wolves. Who plays the boy?

665) Ned Beatty is raped in what film?

666) Laurence Olivier and Michael Caine try to humiliate each other in what mystery?

. . . Answers

658. *Blue Collar*

659. *The Duelists*

660. *Bus Stop*

661. *The Long Riders*

662. c

663. Rosalind Russell

664. Sabu

665. *Deliverance*

666. *Sleuth*

667) In what sci-fi movie is a team of doctors on a submarine miniaturized and sent coursing through the human blood stream?

668) Who plays the woman who takes an interest in Cliff Robertson in *Charly*?

669) Who plays the tough law professor in *The Paper Chase*?

670) In *Mommie Dearest,* who stars as Joan Crawford?

671) In what film does a young man make his fiancée pass a sports trivia test before he will marry her?

672) Who plays Gregory Peck's daughter in *To Kill a Mockingbird*?

673) Which of the following movies never won the Academy Award for Best Picture?
    a. *Marty*
    b. *The Godfather Part II*
    c. *Boys Town*
    d. *Oliver*
    e. *Ordinary People*

674) Who plays the kleptomaniac prisoner in *The Last Detail*?

. . . Answers

667. *Fantastic Voyage*

668. Claire Bloom

669. John Houseman

670. Faye Dunaway

671. *Diner*

672. Mary Badham

673. c

674. Randy Quaid

QUESTIONS

675) What 1949 film based on an Ayn Rand novel features Gary Cooper as an architect who destroys his own building?

676) In what film does Frederic March play a thief being hunted down by police inspector Charles Laughton?

677) Ruby Keeler plays the stand-in who becomes a star in *Forty-Second Street*. True or false?

678) Who are the three female leads in *9 to 5*?

679) What *New Yorker* writer/humorist appears with Robert Walker and Donna Reed in *See Here, Private Hargrove*?

680) Peter Bogdanovich's salute to early screwball comedies stars Barbra Streisand, Ryan O'Neal and Madeline Kahn. Name this film.

681) Who is the object of an assassination attempt in *The Day of the Jackal*?

682) *Oliver's Story* is the sequel to what movie?

683) Who was the director of *Jules and Jim*?

684) What Japanese sci-fi movie features a puddle of radioactive slime that lives in sewers and sucks up passersby?

. . . *Answers*

675. *The Fountainhead*

676. *Les Miserables*

677. True

678. Dolly Parton, Jane Fonda and Lily Tomlin

679. Robert Benchley

680. *What's Up, Doc?*

681. Charles De Gaulle

682. *Love Story*

683. Francois Truffaut

684. *The H-Man*

685) Glenda Jackson won the Oscar for Best Actress for what film?

686) Who plays David Copperfield as a child in the 1935 version of the film?

687) Clint Eastwood is The Good, and Lee Van Cleef is The Bad. Who is The Ugly?

688) Art Carney won an Oscar for playing Harry in *Harry and Tonto*. Who was Tonto?

689) Who is *The Lemon Drop Kid*?

690) Billy Dee Williams stars in *Blacula*. True or false?

691) Gregory Peck portrays what famous outlaw in *The Gunfighter*?

692) In *Kiss of Death*, with Victor Mature, who plays the grinning villain who pushes a crippled old woman down a flight of stairs?

693) Identify the speaker and the film from this line: "Shall we play a game?"

694) *The Creature from the Black Lagoon* was filmed in 3-D. True or false?

. . . Answers

685. *A Touch of Class*

686. Freddie Bartholomew

687. Eli Wallach

688. His cat

689. Bob Hope

690. False (William Marshall)

691. Johnny Ringo

692. Richard Widmark

693. The computer and *Wargames*

694. True

695) John Wayne does not appear in which of these films?

    a. *Rio Lobo*
    b. *Rio Grande*
    c. *Rio Conchos*
    d. *Rio Bravo*

696) Who won an Oscar for Best Acress for *Alice Doesn't Live Here Anymore*?

697) Name the movie and the actor from this line: "I'm mad as hell and I'm not going to take it anymore!"

698) With whom does Shirley Temple dance in *Rebecca of Sunnybrook Farm?*

    a. Buddy Ebsen
    b. Bill Robinson
    c. Ray Bolger

699) In what film does David Bowie play an alien trying to find water for his planet?

700) What movie, made in Ireland in 1970, stars Gene Wilder as a dung collector and salesman?

701) *Pygmalion* was remade as a musical in what 1964 film?

702) Peter O'Toole is an English lord who thinks he's Jesus Christ and, later, Jack the Ripper, in what film?

. . . Answers

695. c

696. Ellen Burstyn

697. Peter Finch and *Network*

698. b

699. *The Man Who Fell to Earth*

700. *Quackser Fortune Has a Cousin in the Bronx*

701. *My Fair Lady*

702. *The Ruling Class*

703) Who directed *My Darling Clementine*?
    a. Howard Hawks
    b. John Huston
    c. John Ford
    d. Michael Curtiz

704) *The Pickwick Papers* is based on whose novel?

705) *Dona Flor and Her Two Husbands* was produced in what country?

706) George Lucas directed *American Graffiti*. True or false?

707) In *The Wild One*, Marlon Brando is asked what he's protesting against. What does he reply?

708) Female impersonator Craig Russell gets involved with a pregnant mental patient in what 1977 Canadian film?

709) What Robert Altman film studies the relationship of convalescent home workers Shelley Duvall and Sissy Spacek and painter Janice Rule?

710) Who plays Jaws, the seven-foot, two-inch bad guy in *The Spy Who Loved Me*?

711) What actor plays Inspector Clouseau's boss in *The Return of the Pink Panther*?

. . . Answers

703. c

704. Charles Dickens

705. Brazil

706. True

707. "What d'ya got?"

708. *Outrageous*

709. *Three Women*

710. Richard Kiel

711. Herbert Lom

712) Sidney Poitier won an Oscar in 1967 for *In the Heat of the Night*. True or false?

713) Who plays the Acid Queen in *Tommy*?

714) What supernatural tale features twin brothers, one good and the other evil, in the 1972 film from a Thomas Tryon novel?

715) What Disney film set in Paris involves the kidnapping of a family of felines by a mean butler?

716) The documentary *Blue Water, White Death* studies the behavior of killer whales. True or false?

717) What film, based on a Henry Fielding novel and starring Albert Finney and Susannah York, won an Oscar for Best Picture in 1963?

718) Who plays the boy who becomes attached to his hunting dog in *Old Yeller*?

719) What dancer made his film debut with Judy Garland in 1942 in *For Me and My Gal*?

720) In *The Wind and the Lion*, who plays the woman kidnapped by sheik Sean Connery?

721) James Caan plays what character in *Rollerball*?

. . . Answers

712. False

713. Tina Turner

714. *The Other*

715. *The Aristocats*

716. False (great white sharks)

717. *Tom Jones*

718. Tommy Kirk

719. Gene Kelly

720. Candice Bergen

721. Jonathan

QUESTIONS

722) Alan Bates and Dirk Bogarde star in a filmization of Bernard Malamud's novel of a Russian peasant wrongly imprisoned. Name this 1968 film.

723) Who stars as *The Boston Strangler*?

724) *The Last Hurrah* was loosely based on whose life?

725) Peter O'Toole and Richard Burton star in what film about the tempestuous friendship between King Henry II and the Archbishop of Canterbury?

726) Who stars as the Russian spy in the 007 film *From Russia With Love*?

727) In what movie does ad man Jack Lemmon pretend that he's married to his luscious neighbor (Romy Schneider) rather than his real wife?

728) Billy Wilder's *Love in the Afternoon* features a romance between middle-aged Gary Cooper and the young daughter of detective Maurice Chevalier. Who plays the daughter?

729) Sean Connery plays the employer of kleptomaniac Tippy Hedren in what film?

730) Who plays Eliza Doolittle's father in *My Fair Lady*?

. . . Answers

722. *The Fixer*

723. Tony Curtis

724. Mayor James Michael Curley of Boston

725. *Becket*

726. Lotte Lenya

727. *Good Neighbor Sam*

728. Audrey Hepburn

729. *Marnie*

730. Stanley Holloway

731) Richard Burton plays a defrocked clergyman in Mexico in what film based on a Tennessee Williams play?

732) Who directed the African big-game film *Rhino*?

733) In *Take Me Out to the Ballgame*, Frank Sinatra and Gene Kelly play for a team owned by whom?

734) Who plays King Arthur in *Camelot*?

735) Robert Blake and Scott Wilson are two young killers who slaughter an unsuspecting family one night in what Truman Capote story?

736) Who plays detective Mo Brummel in *No Way to Treat a Lady*?

737) Name the actress who is the psychotic in *Play Misty for Me*.

738) What band does the score in Woody Allen's *Sleeper*?

739) Sherlock Holmes meets Sigmund Freud in what 1976 movie?

740) Steven Spielberg directed *Star Wars*. True or false?

741) What British comedy ends with a musical crucifix-ion?

. . . Answers

731. *The Night of the Iguana*

732. Ivan Tors

733. Esther Williams

734. Richard Harris

735. *In Cold Blood*

736. George Segal

737. Jessica Walter

738. The Preservation Hall Jazz Band

739. *The Seven Percent Solution*

740. False (George Lucas)

741. *The Life of Brian*

QUESTIONS

742) What is the name of Anthony Hopkins' dummy in *Magic*?

743) Sissy Spacek portrays what country singer in *Coal Miner's Daughter*?

744) Name the character portrayed by Peter Sellers in *Being There*.

745) What was the last movie Marilyn Monroe completed?

746) Richard Burton is the psychiatrist in *Equus*. True or false?

747) Robert Redford is an intelligence agent who learns he is about to be "hit," and Faye Dunaway befriends him in what movie?

748) Who plays Brooke Shields' mother in *Pretty Baby*?

749) What event is recreated in the star-studded film *The Longest Day*?

750) Hoagy Carmichael plays a pianist in the film *To Have and Have Not*. What is his character's name?

751) James Garner plays the leader of these elite World War II troops in what movie?

. . . *Answers*

742. Fats

743. Loretta Lynn

744. Chance the Gardener or Chauncey Gardner

745. *The Misfits*

746. True

747. *Three Days of the Condor*

748. Susan Sarandon

749. The invasion of Normandy in World War II

750. Cricket

751. *Darby's Rangers*

752) John Garfield and Lana Turner are lovers who murder Turner's husband in an adaptation of what James M. Cain novel?

753) Who are the lovers in *Sophie's Choice*?

754) Martin Ritt directed what film about a blacklisted writer?

755) Who plays the heavily sweatered psychiatrist in *Ordinary People*?

756) In *All That Jazz*, Roy Scheider plays a character that is based on the experiences of director Bob Fosse. Name the character.

757) What is the name of the officer played by Marlon Brando in *Apocalypse Now*?

758) Name four of the five characters played by Frank Morgan in *The Wizard of Oz*.

759) Identify the actor and the movie from this line: "If he'd pay me what he's paying them to make me stop robbing him, I'd stop robbing him."

760) Who plays the lead role in the film *Calamity Jane*?

761) Who plays the star pitcher in *The Bad News Bears*?

. . . Answers

752. *The Postman Always Rings Twice*

753. Meryl Streep and Kevin Kline

754. *The Front*

755. Judd Hirsch

756. Joe Gideon

757. Colonel Kurtz

758. a. the Wizard
    b. the Fortune-teller
    c. the Guard at the entrance to Oz
    d. the Soldier at the door leading to the Wizard
    e. the Carriage Driver of "the horse of a different color" in Oz proper

759. Paul Newman in *Butch Cassidy and the Sundance Kid*

760. Doris Day

761. Tatum O'Neal

762) She plays the possessed little girl in *The Exorcist*. Who is she?

763) What actor is Olivia De Havilland's boyfriend in *Hush . . . Hush, Sweet Charlotte*?

764) What is the name of the turkey in the 1961 comedy *All Hands on Deck*, which stars Pat Boone and Buddy Hackett?

765) *Chariots of the Gods*, about visitors from other planets, is based on whose book?

766) Idyllic Shangri-La appears in what film?

767) Gary Grant and Irene Dunne divorce and then plan to wreck each other's upcoming marriage in what 1937 film?

768) In the comedy *Here Comes Mr. Jordan*, Robert Montgomery is the boxer who dies before his time. What instrument is he fond of playing?
    a. trumpet
    b. clarinet
    c. saxophone
    d. bassoon
    e. castinet

769) Who plays the soldier blinded in a Japanese attack in *Pride of the Marines*?

. . . Answers

762. Linda Blair

763. Joseph Cotton

764. Owasso

765. Erich Von Daniken

766. *Lost Horizon*

767. *The Awful Truth*

768. c

769. John Garfield

QUESTIONS

770) Joan Blondell, Bette Davis and Ann Dvorak are childhood friends who renew their ties after going their separate ways in what 1932 film?

771) Who won an Oscar for her portrayal of a self-sacrificing mother in *Mildred Pierce*?

772) *The Heat's On* in 1943 was what Hollywood sexpot's last feature film until the 1979 film *Sextette*?

773) Teenage Shirley Temple got her first "real" kiss on-screen in what movie?

774) Bruce Dern and Walter Matthau are cops searching for a murderer of several bus passengers in what 1974 film?

775) Identify the actor and the movie from this line: "One Rocco more or less isn't worth dying for."

776) What is the name of the villain in *Treasure Island*?

777) Paul Newman and Joel Grey star in the film *Buffalo Bill and the Indians or . . .* What is the remainder of the title?

778) Who plays the title role in *Camille*?

779) The son of Errol Flynn stars in *The Son of Captain Blood*. True or false?

. . . *Answers*

770. *Three on a Match*

771. Joan Crawford

772. Mae West

773. *Kiss and Tell*

774. *The Laughing Policeman*

775. Humphrey Bogart in *Key Largo*

776. Long John Silver

777. *Sitting Bull's History Lesson*

778. Greta Garbo

779. True (Sean Flynn)

780) Who plays the American reporter who gets involved with Nazi spies in Hitchcock's *Foreign Correspondent*?

781) What musical group is the star of the 1978 documentary *The Kids Are Alright*?

782) In what movie did Elizabeth Taylor and Eddie Fisher appear together?

783) Lee Marvin and Clint Eastwood share a wife in *Paint Your Wagon*. Who plays the wife?

784) Who does Shelley Winters portray in *Bloody Mama*?

785) Who plays the G.I. who looks after the orphan in *Dondi*?

786) Charlton Heston won an Oscar for playing *Ben Hur*. Ben Hur was his character's surname. What was Ben Hur's Christian name?

787) Who plays the lead in the 1938 film *Marie Antoinette*?
    a. Norma Shearer
    b. Anita Louise
    c. Luise Rainer
    d. Josephine Hull

. . . Answers

780. Joel McCrea

781. The Who

782. *Butterfield 8*

783. Jean Seberg

784. Ma Barker

785. David Jansen

786. Judah

787. a

788) Before his TV series, James Arness was the star of the 1953 movie *Gunsmoke*. True or false?

789) Who is mistaken for a war hero in Preston Sturges' 1944 satire *Hail the Conquering Hero*?

790) Priest Bing Crosby and nun Ingrid Bergman raise money to build a new church in what movie?

791) Who is the lead actor in the 1948 movie *If You Knew Susie*?

792) Who plays James Stewart's wife in *Strategic Air Command*?

793) Who stars as a just-released convict returning to his wife (Lee Remick) and child in *Baby, the Rain Must Fall*?

794) What British singer appears with Fred Astaire in the 1968 musical *Finian's Rainbow*?

795) Frank Sinatra stars in a biographical film about entertainer Joe E. Lewis. Name the film.

796) Who stars as the super swashbuckler in the film *The Mark of Zorro*?

797) Audrey Hepburn won her first Oscar as a princess longing for a normal life and having a fling with reporter Gregory Peck in what movie?

. . . Answers

788. False (Audie Murphy starred)

789. Eddie Bracken

790. *The Bells of St. Mary's*

791. Eddie Cantor

792. June Allyson

793. Steve McQueen

794. Petula Clark

795. *The Joker Is Wild*

796. Tyrone Power

797. *Roman Holiday*

798) *Merrill's Marauders*, a World War II movie set in Burma, stars what actor in his last screen appearance?

799) *Stop! Look! and Laugh!* is a collection of scenes from some of the top Three Stooges shorts. Name the two hosts of this compilation.

800) Rod Steiger stars as a man covered with tattoos, each one representing a different life experience, in what movie?

801) Rhonda Fleming stars as an infamous belly dancer in the 1890s in what film?

802) Who plays the head of the family in *God's Little Acre*?

803) Who captains the submarine in *Voyage to the Bottom of the Sea*?

804) What rock and roll singer co-stars with Jack Lemmon in the 1960 film *The Wackiest Ship in the Army*?

805) Who plays Thomas Jefferson in *1776*?

806) Who plays the hooker in Clint Eastwood's *The Gauntlet*?

807) What is the name of the advertising agency in *Putney Swope*?

. . . *Answers*

798. Jeff Chandler

799. Paul Winchell and his dummy Jerry Mahoney

800. *The Illustrated Man*

801. *Little Egypt*

802. Robert Ryan

803. Walter Pidgeon

804. Ricky Nelson

805. Ken Howard

806. Sondra Locke

807. Truth and Soul

808) Who stars as the noncommissioned officer in the 1930 movie *All Quiet on the Western Front*?

809) Who stars in the film *Emperor Jones*?

810) Who plays the prim English butler in the 1934 film *Thank You Jeeves*?

811) Peter O'Toole stars as an obsessed, manipulative director in what 1980 drama?

812) The film *Murderer's Row* is about the 1929 New York Yankees. True or false?

813) What is the title of Audie Murphy's autobiography?

814) Who is the skating star of the 1936 movie *One in a Million*?

815) *Harvey*, a six-foot rabbit, was specifically what kind of an apparition?

816) What was the first James Bond film not to star Sean Connery?

817) Red Skelton was the Fuller Brush Man. Who was the Fuller Brush Girl?

818) In *Duel in the Sun*, starring Joseph Cotton and Gregory Peck, who plays the sexy half-breed?

. . . Answers

808. Louis Wolheim

809. Paul Robeson

810. Arthur Treacher

811. *The Stunt Man*

812. False (It's a Matt Helm movie)

813. *To Hell and Back*

814. Sonja Heine

815. A pooka

816. *Casino Royale*

817. Lucille Ball

818. Jennifer Jones

819) Al Pacino is a cop who goes undercover to find a murderer of homosexuals in New York City in what film?

820) What singer plays the feature role in *The Great Caruso*?

821) Who plays Pauline White in the 1947 version of *The Perils of Pauline*?

822) What breed of canine stars in *Lad: A Dog*?

823) What TV German starred as the mass murderer in the 1961 movie *Operation Eichmann*?

824) Mel Gibson recreates his role from *Mad Max* in what 1982 movie?

825) In *Some Like It Hot*, what was Joe E. Brown's response to Jack Lemmon when in the final scene Lemmon tells him they can't get married because he (Lemmon) is really a man?

826) What do Bill Cosby and Raquel Welch do in *Mother, Jugs & Speed*?

827) Who is Harrison Ford's leading lady in *Raiders of the Lost Ark*?

828) Who plays country-western singer Hank Williams in *Your Cheatin' Heart*?

. . . Answers

819. *Cruising*

820. Mario Lanza

821. Betty Hutton

822. A collie

823. Werner Klemperer

824. *The Road Warrior*

825. "Nobody's perfect"

826. They are ambulance workers

827. Karen Allen

828. George Hamilton

QUESTIONS

829) Who plays the female lead in *You Light Up My Life*?

830) *Words And Music*, with Mickey Rooney and Tom Drake, is a biography of what great songwriting team?

831) What is the name of the Dog Who Saved Hollywood?

832) Who stars as the ex-Rebel officer in the western *Sugarfoot*?

833) In *The Great Dictator*, Charlie Chaplin plays two characters. One is the dictator. What is the other?

834) Richard Widmark and Sidney Poitier star in what 1964 Viking adventure?

835) In *Duck Soup*, Trentino (Louis Calhern) hurls three consecutive insults at Rufus T. Firefly (Groucho Marx). What are the three insults?

836) In *Ensign Pulver*, Robert Walker, Jr. performs an operation on Captain Burl Ives and inserts something in Ives' stomach. What did he put in?

837) Lee J. Cobb plays a Chinese warlord in *The Left Hand of God*. True or false?

838) What aficionado of female flesh directed *Beyond the Valley of the Dolls*?

. . . *Answers*

829. Didi Conn

830. Rodgers and Hart

831. *Won Ton Ton*

832. Randolph Scott

833. A ghetto barber

834. *The Long Ships*

835. Worm, swine and upstart

836. Marbles

837. True

838. Russ Meyer

839) Rex Harrison "talks to the animals" in what musical fantasy?

840) Who plays Anne Bancroft's daughter in *The Graduate*?

841) In the original motion picture *The Odd Couple*, who plays Felix and Oscar?

842) Rock Hudson, convinced he's going to die, asks his best friend to find wife Doris Day a new husband in *Send Me No Flowers*. Who is his best friend?

843) What group is the subject and star of *Can't Stop the Music*?

844) *Help!* was the Beatles' first film. True or false?

845) Warren Beatty is a struggling comedian being pursued by the mob in what off-beat film?

846) Kathryn Grayson and Howard Keel star in what musical that includes the songs "Old Man River" and "Can't Help Loving That Man"?

847) What character does Bette Davis play in *A Pocketful of Miracles*?

848) Burt Lancaster is an Indian scout helping the cavalry to capture a renegade Apache in what 1972 Robert Aldrich film?

... *Answers*

839. *Dr. Doolittle*

840. Katherine Ross

841. Jack Lemmon and Walter Matthau

842. Tony Randall

843. The Village People

844. False (*A Hard's Day Night*)

845. *Mickey One*

846. *Show Boat*

847. Apple Annie

848. *Ulzana's Raid*

849) In what 1962 Otto Preminger film about wheeling and dealing in Washington do Charles Laughton, Walter Pidgeon and Henry Fonda star?

850) Convict Robert Stroud is played by what actor in *Birdman of Alcatraz*?

851) Marlon Brando plays an ambassador whose arrival in an Asian country touches off riots in what 1963 movie?

852) *Mirage*, with Diane Baker and Gregory Peck, was directed by Alfred Hitchcock. True or false?

853) What does Jack Lemmon do for a living in *How to Murder Your Wife*?

854) James Stewart and Doug McClure star in a film of a family affected by the Civil War. Name this film which later became a Broadway musical.

855) The French Resistance tries to keep the Germans from stealing many of their national art treasures in what movie which stars Burt Lancaster and Paul Scofield?

856) Michael Caine rose to stardom playing a lecherous playboy who grows tired of his lifestyle in what 1966 movie?

857) Who stars as the Olympic athlete in the 1979 movie *Goldengirl*?

. . . *Answers*

849. *Advise and Consent*

850. Burt Lancaster

851. *The Ugly American*

852. False (Edward Dmytryk)

853. He's a cartoonist

854. *Shenandoah*

855. *The Train*

856. *Alfie*

857. Susan Anton

858) Doris Day and Rod Taylor star in *The Glass Bottom Boat*. What radio and TV crooner plays Day's father?

859) Barbara Eden gets her revenge on a group of citizens who have deemed her an unfit mother in what film?

860) What country is the setting for *The Sound of Music*?

861) What character does Dick Van Dyke play in *Mary Poppins*?

862) What cartoon character is the star of *1001 Arabian Nights*?

863) Rosalind Russell and Janet Blair are Ohio girls who move to Greenwich Village in what 1962 film?

864) Who is Fred Astaire's dancing partner in the 1941 musical *You'll Never Get Rich*?
    a. Ginger Rogers
    b. Rita Hayworth
    c. Cyd Charisse
    d. Leslie Caron

865) In *Picnic*, William Holden visits old friend Cliff Robertson in Kansas and steals his girl away. Who plays the girl?

866) Who played Kate Hepburn's defendant in *Adam's Rib*?

. . . Answers

858. Arthur Godfrey

859. *Harper Valley P. T.A*

860. Austria

861. Bert the Chimney Sweep

862. Mr. Magoo

863. *My Sister Eileen*

864. b

865. Kim Novak

866. Judy Holliday

QUESTIONS

867) In *Born Yesterday*, millionaire Broderick Crawford gets William Holden to tutor his girlfriend. What business was Crawford in?
    a. Bootlegging
    b. Insurance
    c. Handicapping
    d. Junk-dealing

868) Farmer Van Heflin goes after a killer in the 1957 western *3:10 to Yuma*. Who plays the killer?

869) In what movie does Howard Cosell appear to do play-by-play of a couple making love?

870) In *Pennies From Heaven* (1936), Bing Crosby sings the title song but the studio dubbed in Maurice Chevalier's voice. True or false?

871) Who is James Stewart's defendant in *Anatomy of a Murder*?

872) What is the name of Bogart's tank in *Sahara*?

873) Sterling Hayden is the crazed general in *Dr. Strangelove or: How I Learned to Stop Worrying and Love the Bomb*. He admits to having relations with women, but what does he deny them?

874) Who is the star of *Cover Girl*?

. . . *Answers*

867. d

868. Glenn Ford

869. *Bananas*

870. False

871. Ben Gazzara

872. Lulubelle

873. His "essence"

874. Rita Hayworth

875) The following songs are from what film: "The Lady Is a Tramp" and "Bewitched, Bothered and Bewildered"?

876) In the 1973 musical documentary *Wattstax*, who is "Black Moses"?

877) What 1939 movie features Cary Grant as a mail pilot in South America?

878) What serial hero is billed as the "Master of the Stratosphere"?

879) Who play the two fiendish murderers hiding out in the old ladies' Brooklyn house in Frank Capra's *Arsenic and Old Lace*?

880) Frederic March plays the lead in *Anthony Adverse*. True or false?

881) Name Peter Lorre's character in *The Maltese Falcon*.

882) The sleazy Mexican villain in *Virginia City* is played by Humphrey Bogart. True or false?

883) What former TV spy plays the bad guy in *Superman III*?

884) Robert Duvall stars as a down-and-out country-western singer in what film?

. . . *Answers*

875. *Pal Joey*

876. Isaac Hayes

877. *Only Angels Have Wings*

878. Captain Video

879. Raymond Massey and Peter Lorre

880. True

881. Joel Cairo

882. True

883. Robert Vaughn

884. *Tender Mercies*

QUESTIONS

885) Charles Boyer and Peter O'Toole plan to heist an expensive sculpture from a Paris museum in what 1966 movie?

886) Who co-stars with Paul Newman and Sophia Loren in *Lady L*?

887) Marilyn Monroe once appeared in a Marx Brothers movie. True or false?

888) Who stars as the navy nurse in *South Pacific*?

889) Frank Sinatra is a POW who leads a mass escape by hijacking a freight train in what film?

890) In a 1935 musical, Fred Astaire danced with Shirley Temple. True or false?

891) What 1979 musical stars John Savage as an Okie who gets involved with some "far-out" people in NY before his induction into the service?

892) George Hamilton is Dracula in *Love at First Bite*. Who play his lover and his servant?

893) Robert Redford is a warden attempting prison reform in what film?

894) Who plays the obese one in *Fatso*?

895) Who said, "Beelzebub, I've been hoodwinked!"?

. . . Answers

885. *How to Steal a Million*

886. David Niven

887. True (*Love Happy*)

888. Mitzi Gaynor

889. *Von Ryan's Express*

890. False

891. *Hair*

892. Susan St. James and Arte Johnson

893. *Brubaker*

894. Dom DeLuise

895. W.C. Fields

QUESTIONS

896) What comedian plays the gas-station owner in *The Jerk*?

897) What 1976 drama starring Faye Dunaway, Lee Grant and Sam Wanamaker tells the true story of a ship-load of Jewish refugees who are forced to return to Germany when no country will let them land?

898) Laurel and Hardy join the Foreign Legion in what movie?

899) In what movie does Burt Lancaster seize control of a missile base and threaten to launch the bombs at Russia?

900) Kim Novak is a witch in *Bell, Book and Candle*. True or false?

901) What 1967 film featured Spencer Tracy's last appearance?

902) Alan Arkin plays a deaf mute in a small Southern town in what film?

903) What actor is featured in *Barabbas*?

904) In 1937 Walt Disney won a special Academy Award for *Snow White and the Seven Dwarfs*. What star presented him the award?

905) What is Ernest Borgnine's profession in *Marty*?

. . . Answers

896. Jackie Mason

897. *Voyage of the Damned*

898. *The Flying Deuces*

899. *Twilight's Last Gleaming*

900. True

901. *Guess Who's Coming to Dinner?*

902. *The Heart is a Lonely Hunter*

903. Anthony Quinn

904. Shirley Temple

905. He's a butcher

906) Who plays the only British commando to survive after blowing up *The Bridge on the River Kwai*?

907) What is being contested in the 1963 film *The Prize*?

908) The crocodile in *Peter Pan* swallowed something that warns when it is lurking around. What did it swallow?

909) Who stars as Porgy in *Porgy and Bess*?

910) After the Tarzan movies, Johnny Weissmuller starred as a similar character in sixteen films. Name this character.

911) Who plays Bogart's brother in *They Drive by Night*?
    a. James Cagney
    b. Paul Muni
    c. John Garfield
    d. George Raft

912) Peter Lorre stars in *The Beast With Five Fingers*. What is this beast?

913) Robert Alda stars as what composer in *Rhapsody in Blue*?

914) What former Hollywood couple appeared together in 1938 in *Brother Rat*, and again in 1940 in *Brother Rat and a Baby*?

. . . Answers

906. Jack Hawkins

907. The Nobel Prize

908. An alarm clock

909. Sidney Poitier

910. Jungle Jim

911. d

912. A severed hand

913. George Gershwin

914. Ronald Reagan and Jane Wyman

915) Columbia dubbed Al Jolson's voice for Larry Parks in *The Jolson Story*. True or false?

916) In what movie did Paul Henreid light up two cigarettes at once, one for Bette Davis?

917) George Romero's *Night of the Living Dead* takes place outside what city?

918) Bing Crosby is transported back to the days of Camelot in what movie?

919) Toshiro Mifune and Lee Marvin, World War II enemies, are stranded on a desert island in what film?

920) Who plays the rotten magician in *The Geisha Boy*?

921) Which of the following was the first Frankie Avalon and Annette Funicello movie?
    a. *Beach Blanket Bingo*
    b. *Beach Party*
    c. *Muscle Beach Party*
    d. *On The Beach*

922) In the 1939 *Beau Geste*, Gary Cooper, Robert Preston and Ray Milland are the brothers. Who plays the sadistic sergeant major?

923) Who plays Scrooge in the 1951 film *A Christmas Carol*?

. . . *Answers*

915. True

916. *Now, Voyager*

917. Pittsburgh

918. *A Connecticut Yankee in King Arthur's Court*

919. *Hell in the Pacific*

920. Jerry Lewis

921. b

922. Brian Donlevy

923. Alistair Sim

924) Who teaches Kelly Reno about riding in *The Black Stallion*?

925) Tough Marine sergeant John Wayne has a major donnybrook with which of his soldiers in *Sands of Iwo Jima*?

926) Ray Milland is a scientist with the ability to see through objects in what movie?

927) Steve McQueen and Edward G. Robinson are two card sharks who confront each other in what film?

928) Who leads the survivors of a plane wreck out of the desert in *Sands of the Kalahari*?

929) Gilda Radner made a film of her Broadway show. Name it.

930) Who stars and directs *The Last Remake of Beau Geste*?

931) Name the detective that Margaret Rutherford plays in *Murder Most Foul*?

932) Who is the featured actor in *Pumping Iron*?

933) Identify the speaker and the movie from this line: "Calling it your job don't make it right, boss."

934) What two actresses won Oscars for *The Miracle Worker*?

. . . Answers

924. Mickey Rooney

925. Forrest Tucker

926. *X — The Man with the X-ray Eyes*

927. *The Cincinnati Kid*

928. Stuart Whitman

929. *Gilda Live*

930. Marty Feldman

931. Miss Marple

932. Arnold Schwarzenegger

933. Paul Newman in *Cool Hand Luke*

934. Patty Duke and Anne Bancroft

935) In what movie is the song "White Christmas" first heard?

936) Roland Young is haunted by playful ghosts in what movie?

937) In the 1962 film *Ride the High Country*, who play the two aging gunfighters who are reunited for one last job?

938) Identify the speaker and the movie from this line: "We'll always have Paris."

939) Gene Wilder and Richard Pryor team up for hi-jinks on a cross-country train in what film?

940) Which actor has not played the part of D'Artagnan in some version of *The Three Musketeers*?
    a. Gene Kelly
    b. Harry Ritz
    c. Michael York

941) Peter Bogdanovich directed a film about life in a small Texas town in which both Cloris Leachman and Ben Johnson won Oscars. Name the film.

942) *The Sea Wolf* stars Edward G. Robinson as a ship captain. What was his name?

943) In what film do giant ants run rampant?

. . . *Answers*

935. *Holiday Inn*

936. *Topper*

937. Randolph Scott and Joel McCrea

938. Ingrid Bergman in *Casablanca*

939. *Silver Streak*

940. b

941. *The Last Picture Show*

942. Wolf Larsen

943. *Them!*

944) Which Hitchcock film does not star James Stewart?
   a. *Rope*
   b. *Vertigo*
   c. *The Trouble with Harry*

945) Gabe Kaplan directed *Fast Break*. True or false?

946) What song played at the end of *Dr. Strangelove*?

947) In *Kelly's Heroes*, who plays the conniving sergeant?

948) In *Eating Raoul*, what do the murdered bodies end up as?

949) What item of Lee Remick's clothing disappears and later turns up in court in *Anatomy of a Murder*?

950) Who directed the 1959 movie *Samson and Delilah*?

951) Who plays John Wayne's best friend in the Howard Hawks western *Red River*?

952) Name the female leads in both versions of *To Be or Not to Be*.

953) Who narrates the 1966 documentary *John F. Kennedy: Years of Lightning, Day of Drums*?

954) Scientist Gene Barry discovers a synthetic chemical that destroys the invaders in *The War of the Worlds*. True or false?

... Answers

944. c

945. False (Jack Smight)

946. "We'll Meet Again"

947. Don Rickles

948. Dog food

949. Her panties

950. Cecil B. DeMille

951. Walter Brennan

952. Carole Lombard and Anne Bancroft

953. Gregory Peck

954. False (They died from prolonged exposure to our air)

955) What is the name of the country that declared war on America in the movie *The Mouse That Roared*?

956) Jack Lemmon won an Oscar for Best Actor for portraying a dress manufacturer in what film?

957) Who play *Little Fauss and Big Halsy*?

958) What was Farley Granger's profession in *Strangers on a Train*?

959) In what film did Abbott and Costello perform their "Who's on First" routine?

960) Who played George M. Cohan in *Yankee Doodle Dandy*?

961) In the 1948 movie *Sitting Pretty*, Clifton Webb plays a genuis who takes a baby-sitting job. Name his character.

962) Who plays the high school guidance counselor in *Pretty Maids All in a Row*?

963) In H.G. Wells' *The Time Machine*, what character did Yvette Mimieux play?

964) What is the name of Inspector Clouseau's manservant?

. . . Answers

955. The Duchy of Grand Fenwick

956. *Save the Tiger*

957. Michael J. Pollard and Robert Redford

958. A tennis pro

959. *The Naughty Nineties*

960. James Cagney

961. Mr. Belvedere

962. Rock Hudson

963. Weena

964. Kato

965) In which movie did Woody Allen's family live under a roller coaster?

    a. *Love and Death*

    b. *Bananas*

    c. *Annie Hall*

    d. *Take the Money and Run*

966) Who wrote the score to *An American in Paris*?

967) In the film *In the Heat of the Night*, from what city did Sidney Poitier come?

968) George Sanders plays the lead in what eerie movie based on an Oscar Wilde story?

969) Deborah Kerr made her American film debut in what 1947 movie featuring Clark Gable and Sydney Greenstreet?

970) Gary Burghoff is the only actor to appear in both the film and TV versions of *M*A*S*H*. True or false?

971) Who directed *Pat Garrett and Billy the Kid*?

972) Who won an Oscar as the deaf mute in *Johnny Belinda*?

973) Identify the speaker and the movie from this line: "What this country needs is a good seven-cent nickel."

974) Who plays James Earl Jones' mistress in *The Great White Hope*?

. . . Answers

965. c

966. George Gershwin

967. Philadelphia

968. *The Picture of Dorian Gray*

969. *The Hucksters*

970. True

971. Sam Peckinpah

972. Jane Wyman

973. Groucho Marx in *Animal Crackers*

974. Jane Alexander

975) What did Richard Chamberlain do for a living in *The Last Wave*?

976) Greer Garson won an Oscar for her performance in *Random Harvest*. True or false?

977) Lina Wertmuller directed a film in which a sailor and a wealthy woman are stranded on an island and undergo dramatic changes. Name the film.

978) What was the name of Dustin Hoffman's character in *Midnight Cowboy*?

979) Name the speaker and the film from this quote: "I'll get you, my pretty. And your little dog, too."

980) Name the Seven Dwarfs.

981) What 1941 Raoul Walsh film tells the story of the massacre at Little Big Horn?

982) Dad Walter Huston was directed by son John in *The Treasure of Sierra Madre*. True or false?

983) *Edge of Darkness*, with Errol Flynn and Ann Sheridan, is about an underground against the Nazis in what occupied country?

984) Jane Fonda falls in love with paraplegic veteran John Voight in what film?

. . . Answers

975. He was an attorney

976. False (She won for *Mrs. Miniver*)

977. *Swept Away . . . by an unusual destiny in the blue sea of August*

978. Enrico "Ratso" Rizzo

979. Margaret Hamilton in *The Wizard of Oz*

980. Grumpy, Dopey, Sleepy, Happy, Sneezy, Doc and Bashful

981. *They Died With Their Boots On*

982. True

983. Norway

984. *Coming Home*

985) What film based on a Herman Hesse novel is about an Indian who leaves home to seek adventure?

986) Lauren Bacall hires detective Paul Newman to find her husband in what movie?

987) What food is being harvested by James Cagney and Pat O'Brien in *Torrid Zone*?

988) Jack Benny and Ann Sheridan buy a dilapidated country house in what movie?

989) William Powell plays the eccentric head of the household in the comedy *Life with Father*. Who plays his wife?

990) Who stars as the wheelchair-ridden author in *The Man Who Came to Dinner*?

991) In what Edgar Allen Poe tale does Vincent Price think he is his deceased father, a torturer during the Spanish Inquisition?

992) In *Dr. Ehrlich's Magic Bullet*, Edward G. Robinson is a nineteenth century German doctor searching for a cure to what?
    a. Syphilis
    b. TB
    c. Whooping cough
    d. Measles

. . . Answers

985. *Siddhartha*

986. *Harper*

987. Bananas

988. *George Washington Slept Here*

989. Irene Dunne

990. Monty Woolley

991. *The Pit and the Pendulum*

992. a

993) In *Knute Rockne — All American*, Ronald Reagan tells the team to "win one for the Gipper". True or false?

994) *Always Leave Them Laughing* (1949) stars a comic who went on to become a big success in TV. Name this funny man.

995) Bogart plays Sam Spade in *The Big Sleep*. True or false?

996) Who plays *Machine Gun Kelly* in 1958?

997) In what film is Charlie Chaplin in love with a blind flower girl?

998) *The Molly Maguires* is about a secret society of what?

999) What 1974 Ken Shapiro film is composed of satiric skits about television?

1000) Who plays the dance hall girl who sings "See What the Boys in the Back Room Will Have" in *Destry Rides Again*?

1001) What is the name of the evil queen in *Sleeping Beauty*?

1002) Alan Bates is a professor who hates everything about his and everyone else's life in what Harold Pinter drama?

. . . Answers

993. False (Pat O'Brien said it)

994. Milton Berle

995. False (He plays Philip Marlowe)

996. Charles Bronson

997. *City Lights*

998. Irish mine workers

999. *The Groove Tube*

1000. Marlene Dietrich

1001. Maleficent

1002. *Butley*

1003) Loretta Young and Clark Gable star in what adaptation of a Jack London adventure story?

1004) Who plays Chief Crazy Horse in the movie of the same name?

1005) Groucho Marx appears with what singer in *Copacabana*?

1006) What movie was Orson Welles' followup to *Citizen Kane*?

1007) What is the name of the ship in *The Sea Wolf*?

1008) Elliot Gould and George Segal are compulsive gamblers in what movie?

1009) Who must choose between the church and her love for Doctor Elvis Presley in *Change of Habit*?

1010) Orson Welles and Joan Fontaine star in what Charlotte Bronte adaptation?

1011) Glenn Ford's son tries to find him a wife in *The Courtship of Eddie's Father*. Who plays Eddie?

1012) What Hall of Fame baseball pitcher did Ronald Reagan play?

1013) Katherine Hepburn is a spinster who is romanced by con man Burt Lancaster in what movie?

. . . *Answers*

1003. *Call of the Wild*

1004. Victor Mature

1005. Carmen Miranda

1006. *The Magnificent Ambersons*

1007. The Ghost

1008. *California Split*

1009. Mary Tyler Moore

1010. *Jane Eyre*

1011. Ron Howard

1012. Grover Cleveland Alexander

1013. *The Rainmaker*

1014) Who stars opposite Clark Gable in *Somewhere I'll Find You*, a story about World War II correspondents?

1015) In *The Caine Mutiny*, the crew had a derogatory nickname for Captain Queeg. What was it?

1016) Who stars as the doctor in *Son of Frankenstein*?

1017) What is George C. Scott's character's name in *Dr. Strangelove*?

1018) Who plays the social worker in *Requiem for a Heavyweight*?

1019) Grace Kelly won an Oscar as the wife of alcoholic Bing Crosby in what movie?

1020) Marlon Brando plays a Korean War pilot who falls in love with a Japanese girl in what James Michener story?

1021) In *The Cowboy and the Lady*, Gary Cooper is the cowboy. Who is the lady?

1022) What Disney film features the song "Who's Afraid of the Big Bad Wolf?"

1023) Identify the actor and the movie from this line: "I'm a man who likes talking to a man who likes to talk."

. . . Answers

1014. Lana Turner

1015. "Old Yellow Stain"

1016. Basil Rathbone

1017. General Buck Turgidson

1018. Julie Harris

1019. *The Country Girl*

1020. *Sayonara*

1021. Merle Oberon

1022. *Three Little Pigs*

1023. Sydney Greenstreet in *The Maltese Falcon*

1024) Who is the TV star that got his big break in a movie starring Sylvester Stallone?

1025) Who plays Steve Allen's girlfriend in *The Benny Goodman Story*?

1026) Who is the star of *The Buster Keaton Story*?

1027) What comedy team stars in *The Caddy*?

1028) In *Take Her, She's Mine*, James Stewart plays the harried father of a wild teenager. Who is the teenager?

1029) Doris Day teaches a journalism class and city editor Clark Gable becomes her top student in what film?

1030) In 1951, Gregory Peck portrayed what nineteenth century British naval hero?

1031) Composer Cole Porter is portrayed by Cary Grant in what movie?

1032) Laurence Harvey, Angela Lansbury and Frank Sinatra star in what 1962 film about communists trying to take over the American government?

. . . *Answers*

1024. Mr. T

1025. Donna Reed

1026. Donald O'Connor

1027. Dean Martin and Jerry Lewis

1028. Sandra Dee

1029. *Teacher's Pet*

1030. *Captain Horatio Hornblower*

1031. *Night and Day*

1032. *The Manchurian Candidate*

THE SURVIVALIST SERIES
by Jerry Ahern